DANNY ORLIS
AND THE
MYSTERY AT NORTHWEST HIGH

DANNY ORLIS
AND THE
MYSTERY AT NORTHWEST HIGH

BERNARD PALMER

Please note that several books in the Danny Orlis series are published by Sword of the Lord Publications and are available for purchase on their website, www.swordbooks.com.

Aneko Press Youth

www.anekopress.com

Aneko Press, Life Sentence Publishing, and our logos are trademarks of Life Sentence Publishing, Inc.
203 E. Birch Street
P.O. Box 652
Abbotsford, WI 54405

JUVENILE FICTION / Religious / Christian / Action & Adventure
Paperback ISBN: 979-8-88936-080-3
eBook ISBN: 979-8-88936-081-0
10 9 8 7 6 5 4 3 2 1
Available where books are sold

CONTENTS

CHAPTER 1

GIVE IT A TRY

Two weeks before school began, Kay Orlis drove her foster children, the Davis triplets, to Northwest High to enroll. Each of them carried his birth certificate, transcript of grades, and health record from Fairview.

"I feel like I'm entering kindergarten instead of my senior year," Del grumbled.

Kay laughed. "And you even brought your mommy with you!"

They all were awed by the mammoth, sprawling structure that would be their alma mater for a year. Inside the main lobby, a directory indicated that the registrar's office was room B-34. Then they saw that the corridors were labeled, and corridor B was close to the main entrance.

A pleasant-looking gray-haired lady introduced herself as the registrar's secretary, Miss Lawrence.

The three teens handed her the information they had brought and sat back to wait as she filled out the necessary forms for registering as Northwest High seniors.

After examining the first card, Miss Lawrence looked a little alarmed. She quickly read the others as if to disprove or confirm her sudden suspicion. She looked up from her desk and said, "I'm afraid I have some bad news for you three. You don't have nearly enough credits to graduate this year."

"What?" they exclaimed.

"You all have indicated that you plan to go on to further education, and our college prep course is arranged to provide you with all credits necessary to meet college entrance requirements." Miss Lawrence continued to explain that, according to their system, the triplets needed another year of both English and science, a semester each in art and music, and several electives, besides the normal load they would carry as seniors. They needed two more semesters to fit in all these classes.

Danny could hardly believe the situation as they explained it to him that night at dinner. He shook his head several times as the three told their unhappy account. At last he said, "Well, you'll be ready for college, anyway."

"And a whole lot older," DeeDee added. "I don't want to be the oldest girl in the junior class."

"Then keep your mouth shut," Del advised. "Nobody'll know."

After more discussion and some prayer, the triplets finally accepted the fact that their high school career would be an extra year long.

The week before classes began at Rock Point's Northwest High, Del and Doug reported for football. They were astonished by the size of the squad and the number of coaches. Back in Fairview, where they had lived before moving to Colorado, the football team had a head coach and one assistant. At Northwest, it seemed there were coaches everywhere they looked. There were offensive and defensive coaches, a couple of backfield coaches, and some who did not seem to be responsible for any particular positions.

"I didn't know there were even any colleges that have so many coaches." Del opened the car door on his side and scooted behind the wheel when the orientation meeting was over. "The season'll be over before we learn half their names."

"Did you ever see so many guys out for the team?"

"There were more guys on the field tonight than we used to have in the whole high school in Fairview." They turned in the direction of the house where they and their triplet sister, DeeDee, lived with Danny and Kay Orlis. "You know, we're going to have a rough time making the team."

"Making the team?" Doug echoed. "We'll be lucky if we don't get cut from the squad."

The first week, the coaches were more concerned with getting the guys in condition than they were in scrimmaging. For an hour, the boys worked out and ran laps around the track. That was no problem for Del and Doug. They had been working hard all summer and reported in good condition while most of the others were heavier than they should have been and short of wind. It took some time before they could make it around the track without puffing and had the fat off their middles. The coaches drove them relentlessly, and each day they seemed a little better able to run and tackle than they had been before. At last they were ready for the first scrimmage of the season.

That was what Del and Doug had been waiting for, but they knew they were in for a rough time getting anywhere in football that season when they saw the size of the guys the coaches chose for the first string. They all weighed around two hundred pounds and were at least six feet tall. The Davis boys had to stretch to make five-nine and put rocks in their pockets to weigh one sixty-five. They were well muscled and powerful, but they simply did not have the bulk to impress coaches that were only looking at size.

The head coach, Mr. Knight, had made a little speech at the orientation meeting, telling the squad that no one had his position sewed up – not even the returning starters or the biggest, fastest guys on last year's team.

"You're all going to have to earn your positions." He looked around the locker room, squinting narrowly at them. "I don't care *who* you are."

It made a nice speech, but his actions spoke differently. Or so it seemed to Del and Doug. It looked to them as though he put the biggest, fastest guys on the starting lineup of the first team.

"And we get all the runts on the second team," Doug murmured. He thought he spoke softly enough, so the coaches did not hear him, but one of the assistants spun around quickly.

"What did you say?" he asked menacingly.

The boy's cheeks crimsoned. "Nothing, sir. Nothing at all."

"Just watch the cracks, or you'll be the first to go."

Hurriedly, Doug trotted out onto the field. *Why did I open my big mouth?* he wondered. He sure had not meant anything by it. He had played sports long enough to know a guy did not say or do things to get the coaches down on him – not if he wanted to play.

The scrimmage was as rough and uneven as all first scrimmages are, and the coaches were anxious to see what all the guys could do. The guys streamed on and off the field so fast the Davis boys did not see how as many coaches as Northwest had could even possibly keep track of everyone. Nevertheless, they did their best the few minutes they were in.

Del got off a long, bullet-hard pass that scored a touchdown for the reserves against the regulars, but even that was not enough to attract a favorable nod from the coaches. The whistle blew, and Mr. Knight stomped all over the tackles for not getting in and smearing "the new man" before he carried the ball away.

"You play like that next Friday night, and Milford's going to clobber you." They cringed under his withering glare. "And you'll deserve it!" Then he turned to the ends. "You, Collins! Go up in the air after that ball! What's your trouble? Got lead in your feet?"

The lanky end flushed and muttered something unintelligible. The team lined up for the kickoff with the reserves receiving again.

"This time, look alive!"

The end, mad as a bull, charged in on the receiver as he took the kickoff and drove him to the ground before he moved two steps. On the next play, he did the same before Del could get rid of the ball. Then he shot off a second pass good for long yardage, and on the next he took a handoff for a gain of seven yards over the left tackle.

Again the whistle blew. Again Mr. Knight chewed out the defensive linemen. So it went, throughout the rest of the scrimmage. As long as the first string defensive unit smeared the second team for no gain or a loss, the play continued. Once the reserves ticked off a good gain, and the whistle sounded while a lineman and defensive back were bawled out for failing to play their positions properly. Del was furious as he and Doug drove home that night after practice.

"What good does it do for us to knock ourselves out trying to make the team?" he demanded of his brother. "We don't have a chance."

Doug disagreed. "I'm not giving up yet. Somebody might get hurt or have grade trouble or start to slip a little. I'll hang in there as long as they'll have me on the squad."

"I suppose I will, too, but I think we've got rocks in our heads for doing it," Del retorted pessimistically.

His brother did not reply.

Del signaled a left turn and headed up their street. When he turned off the key, he said, "A lot of good it'll do us to hang in there taking abuse like we did this afternoon. If we do make a good block or throw a pass or pick up some yardage on the ground, it's never because we're any good. It's because someone on the varsity missed an assignment or wasn't digging in." He jerked the door open. "We never get any credit for anything we do! Every one of those coaches must be blind."

"I'm like you this far," Doug said, quietly opening his door. "I do think they're going to stick with last year's regulars if they can. And I don't think we can blame them for that. The guys on the first string have been playing together for two years. It'd be rough for anyone to break in, especially outsiders like you and me."

"Well, I'm about to quit trying." And to emphasize the finality, Del got out and slammed the door.

"Not me. I just want to play. I don't even care whether I earn a letter," Doug said cheerfully as they sauntered toward the house. "Wonder if Kay baked today." He opened the back door. "Yep, she did."

The next few days, the coaches intensified their efforts to whip the team into shape for the Milford game. They introduced a new set of plays to use against the stiff Milford defense and had the second string throwing Milford plays at the varsity defense.

The Davis boys only got to play part of the time, even with the reserves, and Del's temper smoldered. Doug was afraid Del was about to explode, and tried to kid him out of it. "Just think," Doug said with a grin, "if we make it through this, we're a cinch for the Marines!" But Del only scowled.

Both Davis boys continued to put everything they had into the scrimmages the rest of the week, but apparently the coaching staff was not impressed, not even mildly amused. They did not play at all in the final practice session, and Mr. Knight acted as though they were not even there.

Driving home that night, Del raised his voice belligerently. "I don't get it. The harder we try, the worse things get. What gives?"

Doug shrugged expressively.

"I don't know about you, but I've *had* it. I think I'm going to quit."

"Not me. If they get rid of me, they're going to have to kick me out."

Doug did not know how prophetically he spoke. On Thursday before the Milford game, Mr. Knight announced the names of those to be kept in the final squad cut. For the first time, he said he appreciated the work the reserves put in and thanked them all for their efforts. "We thought we would be able to carry the squad at its present size all through the season, but at our last staff meeting, we decided that we can't handle so many. We've gone over the names of all reserves as carefully as we can and have tried to assess your ability. We're probably keeping some we should cut and cutting some we should keep, but we have to take that chance."

After more of the same, he picked up the clipboard with the list of the guys who would be remaining on the football squad. "If your name isn't on this list," he continued, "please turn in your equipment as you leave the locker room after we're done."

Del and Doug relaxed as he read the names. They were both convinced that they would be kept on the squad. As Mr. Knight neared the end of the list, they squirmed uneasily. Then, abruptly he stopped reading.

They had not made it! Not even for the reserves! The frown lines about Del's mouth grew tense. "There must be some mistake!" he murmured fiercely.

But Doug did not agree with him. The coach would never make a mistake about a thing like that. They were dropped from the squad. They would not get to play football at Rock Point that season. And back in Fairview they had starred! That made it all the more incredible! Here, they weren't even good enough to play with the reserves. Collins, one of the regulars who had made it, came over to them, trying hard to keep from showing his own feelings of superiority. "Tough luck. Maybe next year."

"Next year?" Del hurled the words bitterly at him. "Fat chance! I'm not even comin' out next year."

Doug felt as bad as Del did about being dropped from the football squad. In a way, he thought he was even more upset than Del was. It hurt him worse to lose, for some reason. Del wanted to win, but it did not mean all that much. Doug had never seen him cry because he lost a game or missed a tackle or failed to make an important first down. He was not proud of it, but he had cried about a lot of his mistakes. It made Doug so mad at himself that more than once he had felt like quitting. But what really happened was that he had only dug in and tried that much harder the next time.

Now that would not do any good.

"There's nothing we can do about it," Doug told Del the next time he started complaining that they had been handed a raw deal. "There's no need to bellyache anymore."

Del could not forget it so easily. "We didn't even get credit for trying. We learned a new set of plays every week and did our best to run past the varsity. And what thanks do we get? 'Thanks, but we don't need you anymore!' I wish we'd stayed back in Fairview. If we had, we'd be playing every game and knocking off all the competition in sight. *They* appreciated us!"

Doug had to agree with him. They were certainly well accepted back in Fairview. For the first time since Mr. Knight read the list, he began to feel sorry for himself and Del.

* * *

Del and Doug had visited Chuck Grover in the hospital once since school started, and he was so rude, they did not go back. They thought he had been released from the hospital long before and were surprised to learn that he was still there. Right after school started, they received a letter from Scot MacDermott, their foreman at Mr. Kramer's ranch. He told them that Chuck's leg was not improving. The doctor had had to operate and reset the limb. Now Chuck was even in traction. "Strung up in bed like a butchered elk," Scot expressed it.

"That's tough for him," Del said. He thought he really meant it, although he had to admit he did not like Chuck very well. They continued reading the letter, which was scrawled in pencil on notebook paper.

"Kramer said he wished you would of got to him this summer. Now is a good time, too, with Chuck being laid up, missing school and all. Besides, the boy's uncle and me figger you boys to be the ones to bring him around. We're hoping and praying that he'll be listening next time you go. God bless, Scot Mac."

"Sounds like old Scot's a Christian, huh, Del?"

"Yeah. I never guessed he was one of us last summer."

"Neither did I. Wow, we sure blew *that* summer." Doug shook his head and looked back down at the letter. "Want to give Chuck another try?"

"Sure. Anything for old Scot."

CHAPTER 2

HAPPY LANDING

Del and Doug thought some of the guys at school might razz them about getting dropped from the football squad, but nobody said anything. Suddenly, they realized the kids acted as though they might not even know. In a way that made it all the worse. The Davises counted for so little in the big school that nobody paid any attention to them or what they did.

So the two brothers decided they would not even go to the Northwest-Milford game on Friday night; but half an hour before the kickoff, they changed their minds. Actually, it was their sister, DeeDee, who convinced them they ought to go, although they would have been reluctant to admit it.

"You're not going to the game tonight?" she asked, astounded. "It's only the first game, but everyone says it'll decide the conference championship."

"So?" Del exclaimed.

"Just why aren't you going?"

"Why should we, after the way we've been treated?"

"You mean, you're *not* going to the game because Mr. Knight didn't think you could play well enough to help the team?" Contempt thinly etched her voice. "Where's your school spirit?"

"Back in Fairview," Doug answered.

Del shrugged his indifference. "I don't care whether we win tonight or not. It would serve them right if we lose every game."

DeeDee whirled on him. "You sound just like you did when we were little kids. 'If I can't go first, I'm not going to play!' Why don't you grow up?" She put on her coat and buttoned it. "As far as I'm concerned, you both can stay home and pout if you want to. I'm going to go to the football game and enjoy myself."

Doug started to defend himself and Del, but she stormed out the door without listening to him. He looked up at Del. What DeeDee had said had really stung his brother. Doug was glad she had not stayed around to see how much she got to him.

"Well?" Doug asked with a sheepish grin.

"Well, what?" Del was still angry and did not care who knew it. His eyes blazed, and his voice was harsh and explosive.

"Are we goin to 'stay home and pout' or do we go to the game and try to enjoy ourselves?"

"I couldn't have a good time watching that bunch play marbles."

"That's about the way I feel too." Then Doug recalled that look on DeeDee's face and the scorn in her voice. "I don't like getting dropped from the football team any better than you do, but I'm beginning to think DeeDee's right. The big trouble with us is that we're feeling sorry for ourselves."

"We've got good reason to be mad. We got a raw deal." Del headed for the kitchen to raid the cookie jar.

Doug followed his brother out of the living room. "How would *we* feel if we'd made the team and a couple of guys who didn't got mad and refused to come watch us play?"

Del looked briefly at him and then away.

"We'd think they were mighty poor sports, wouldn't we?" Doug prodded.

Del stuffed a big cookie into his mouth. He knew well enough what his brother said was true. That sort of thing happened every year at every school that had enough guys to field a football team. Some of those who did not make it took it well; some got so mad they would not even speak to those who had been good – or lucky – enough to stay on the squad.

But, Del reasoned, *this is different.* He was not bitter toward the guys who made the squad; it was not their fault. He was ticked off at the guys with the whistles. Not one had given him and Doug half a chance. Not only that, no one had given them credit for anything they had done right.

Doug spoke again. "I've been thinking about

something else, Del. Some of the guys who know we got cut will be watching tonight to see if we show up for the game."

"Huh!" His cheeks darkened with embarrassment, but his voice had lost none of its edge. "Nobody at *that* school knows or cares what we do."

Doug shook his head. By this time he was as disgusted with Del as DeeDee had been with both of them a few minutes before. "I'm not hanging around here arguing all night. I'm going to the game. You can sit here alone if you want to."

Still grumbling, Del got his coat and followed his brother outside. He felt silly about going and thought Doug was all wrong, but he did not want to sit home alone all evening.

Shortly after the game started, they began to see why the coaches had been reluctant to introduce changes into the lineup. The guys played like a well-functioning machine, executing each play with the precision of a computer. They had been rough and clumsy during practice, but now that they were playing for keeps, all of that was behind them.

Even the substitutes played their positions smoothly, meshing in with the rest of the team better than Del or Doug could possibly have done. They both realized it as they watched the first half.

Milford was good, and they, too, were determined. But they were not good enough. In eight plays following the opening kickoff, Northwest marched sixty-seven yards and punched the ball across for the first score. Before the half ended, Northwest led twenty-one to nothing.

"I've never seen high school guys play like our guys did the first half." Doug exclaimed, admiration creeping into his voice. "Did you see Collins? He's great!"

Del's praise was less enthusiastic, but he had to admit that they were good. "They sure didn't look this sharp in practice," he muttered.

"I've got to agree with that, but they're really showing us some football tonight." Doug paused significantly. "Now I can see why Mr. Knight wouldn't give you and me a second look. We just don't have it the way those guys do."

"Yeah." For some reason, Del felt a little better after that. Anyone watching Northwest that night could see why the squad was so small. He did not feel so bad being beaten out by guys who could play like that.

Milford stiffened briefly at the start of the third quarter and worked the ball down to the Northwest nineteen-yard line. There the defensive unit came alive and drove Milford back fourteen yards on three successive plays before swarming in to block the attempted field goal. That took the heart out of the Milford eleven. They only went through the motions for the rest of the game; they knew they were beaten and played like it. Midway through the third quarter,

Mr. Knight started substituting freely. Before the game was over, everyone on the bench saw action. The final score was 27-0. They set a new record for the biggest win for a first game in Northwest's history.

On the way home, Del and Doug were still talking about the football team and the way they crushed Milford. If the opposition that night was the best in the conference, what good would it do to play the rest of the games? Northwest would only slaughter the other teams. They both felt secretly proud of the victory.

"If they play basketball here the way they play football," Doug said at last, "we won't have a chance there, either."

"Right now, I couldn't care less."

Doug gave his brother a sidelong glance for some clue as to his meaning.

"Basketball never did mean much to me," Del explained.

"It does to me," Doug admitted.

On the curb, Del paused. "There is something I'd really like to do, though. I'd like to get those skis we've been talking about and start skiing. That sounds like fun to me."

Doug's eyes brightened. "You've got yourself a deal!"

They went into the house, their failure to make the team completely forgotten. They began making plans to use part of the money they had earned that summer to buy skis and boots.

The next day, they made a tour of the ski shops trying to find used equipment that would be satisfactory. Neither of them felt they wanted to go to the expense of new equipment.

"It's just as easy to break a leg with a fifty dollar pair of skis as it is a *four hundred* and fifty dollar pair," Del said.

"You're sure optimistic, I can say that for you."

At last they found the equipment they needed at a price they felt they could afford. The clerk tried to interest them in a brief series of lessons, but they were not interested.

"You ought to have somebody show you how," he said with friendly concern.

"The way I figure it," Del said, "there's nothing to learn that a few dozen falls won't teach us."

The next Saturday morning, they borrowed Danny's car and drove up into the snow-clad hills, their skis firmly secured on top.

"You know, the guy in that store was right. We ought to take a few lessons," Doug said.

"I agree, but there's a little thing called money that we don't have much of. If we'd taken those lessons he was trying to sell us, we couldn't have bought the skis and boots."

"You've got a point there. I guess we're better off skiing without lessons than without skis."

Del flashed a quick grin. "Bright boy. I'm glad you're my brother."

"You should be. I'm full of little gems like that."

The boys did not go to a regular commercial run but found a place a few miles from town where they could practice in seclusion. They pulled off the highway onto a small road and stopped near a gentle slope.

"Well, here we are," Doug said, glancing at his brother.

"So I see." He got out of the car and looked around. "And what do we do now?"

"The first thing I'd suggest is that we put our skis on."

"Very funny. And suppose you tell me how we do that?"

"You saw the guy in the store, didn't you?"

"Sure, I saw him. But all I remember is that he put his feet in the boots and clamped the boots to the skis. I sort of think I could've figured that out by myself."

Doug fished a paperback from his pocket. "I have all the answers right here," he said. "Give me a little time, and I'll tell you anything you want to know."

Del came around the car and glanced over Doug's shoulder.

"*How to Ski.* Big deal! I suppose it's one easy lesson."

"This is straight from the pros. Read this book and you'll be ready for the Olympics."

"I'll believe *that* when I see it."

"Don't be so skeptical," Doug told him. "It says here that skiing ought to be easy for you and me. It says, 'Football players find it particularly simple.'"

Del snorted. "According to the coaches at Northwest, we aren't football players – or have you forgotten?"

"Just trying to be helpful."

"Okay, I'll shut up. I just want to learn how to ski."

"Then you came to the right place." Doug turned a few pages. "'How to Carry Your Skis.' Now, that ought to be a good place for us to begin."

Del leaned closer so he could read what the book had to say. "I think the best place for us to begin is by goin' back to town and waiting until we've earned enough money to hire someone to teach us."

Doug straightened. "Lay off, will you? It's all here in the book. All we do is study it. It didn't cost *you* a cent."

"Okay. Okay. Tell me what I'm supposed to do first."

"'Take a look at these diagrams, will you? It's all here."

Del scanned the simplified drawings. "Yeah, I can see just how to do it now. There's nothing to it." He took three steps toward the hill and stopped. "Hang on! We haven't even got our skis on yet!"

Doug shook his head. "Doesn't that beat all?"

"I knew there was something I'd forgotten. It might be a good idea for us to put our skis on before we start walking in them."

"Let's go back to the beginning of the book." Doug flipped back to the first chapter.

"That makes more sense than anything else you've said since we got out here," Del teased.

"You just watch what you say, or I won't let you use my book. Then you'll *never* learn how to ski."

The Davis boys put their skis on, and, using the diagrams in Doug's book as a guide, they took the first step toward mastering the art of skiing. They were not afraid to try. That was in their favor. And they had water skied a lot of times when they lived on the lake near Fairview, Minnesota. But snow skiing was different than anything they had ever done. It seemed to have a technique all its own.

They tried and fell and tried again, laughing at the ridiculously clumsy way they sprawled in the snow. At last, Doug pulled out the instruction book once more.

"Let's read this thing again. We must be missing something."

"We're missing a good teacher."

Doug made a face at his brother as he leafed through the pages. "Wait a minute. Here's a page we need to study. 'How to Fall.'"

"Speak for yourself. I already *know* how to fall. I've been doing it all afternoon."

"This is so you won't get hurt, stupid."

"Now he tells me!" With that, Del threw his hands up, lost his balance, sat in the snow, and listened while his brother read to him "How to Fall."

CHAPTER 3

AN ARRESTING INVITATION

Although Doug and Del agreed that they should go to the hospital and see Chuck Grover right away, they put off going for a couple of weeks. First there had been football practice every night. Then Kay had them raking leaves in their enormous yard every Saturday. Actually, they did not want to go and see Chuck, although they would not admit that, even to themselves. They still might not have gone if Del had not insisted on it.

"Old Scot's probably up at the ranch wondering when he's going to hear from us about our visit to Chuck."

Doug frowned. "I suppose you're right about that, but I'm sure not very anxious to go."

"Neither am I, but we owe it to Scot."

"I know."

"And he'll expect us to talk to the guy about becoming a Christian."

"I've been thinking about that," Doug continued. He began to wonder if this were the real reason he was not too anxious to go and visit Chuck. He did not really want to talk to him about Jesus Christ. "It's sure not going to do any good. Chuck's one guy who just isn't interested. He couldn't care less."

"I know."

Nevertheless, they got ready that evening and went to the hospital. As they went out to the car, Del began to wonder if they had really tried to present Christ to Chuck. DeeDee probably had, but he did not think he and Doug had been concerned enough about him to make any difference in Chuck's life. He could not remember ever having prayed hard for the guy. He had prayed harder about playing football. Del was uneasy and more quiet than usual as he and Doug went to the hospital and picked up passes to Chuck's room.

The boy in the narrow white bed seemed glad to see them. That, in itself, was surprising. The other time they had visited him, he told them they could leave and never come back. This time his grin was broad, and he asked them to sit down.

Del and Doug could not keep from staring at him. He looked worse this time than before. His leg was suspended in the air above the bed, with weights to keep pulling on it. And they could tell he had lost a lot of weight.

"You look as though you've been having trouble," Del said.

"Yeah." Chuck grimaced. "Plenty of it. They operated on it once, and for a while they thought they might have to operate again."

"That's rough."

"We got a letter from Scot a few weeks ago," Doug said. "He told us about it."

Chuck nodded. "He wrote to me that you were coming around to see me, but I'd about given up on you."

"We were busy," Del replied lamely.

"I know." For the first time, that old gleam reflected from the injured boy's eyes. "When you didn't come, I figured that you guys must've quit praying for me."

They eyed him quizzically, trying to decide whether he was taunting them again or if he really meant it. Knowing him, they were suspicious, but the look in his eyes was bewildering. It was hard to make out what he meant.

"As a matter of fact," Del told him, "we *have* been praying for you."

"That's real nice of you." He managed a thin laugh. "That ought to earn you a few brownie points."

"Scot's praying for you too."

At the mention of his uncle's foreman, Chuck's

face lost much of its contempt, and his eyes grew serious. "Why's he praying for me?"

"Same reason we are," Del said. "He loves you, your uncle loves you, and we want you to know that God loves you more than all of us put together."

Chuck looked down at his cast. At first it seemed as though he was halfway interested, then he shook his head. "Sure," he retorted. "God loves me so much He gave me this broken leg."

Del explained that God permitted him to break his leg, but He did not cause it. Like so many things that happen, he told him, his leg was broken because he insisted on getting his own way; and when he did not, he ran away to cause trouble.

Chuck's bitterness came rushing back. "When you get right down to it," he retorted, "it was *your* fault. I was just having a little fun with your sister, and you guys had to lose your cool and make a big deal of it. *You* made me run away!"

Del ignored him and tried to continue, but the opportunity was lost. Chuck was not listening anymore.

Doug, who had taken little part in the conversation up to this point, crossed his legs nervously. Talking to someone like Chuck was always hard.

He wished he and Del were more like DeeDee. She seemed able to talk with anyone about her Savior as easily as though she was talking about a new dress or the party at the church the next weekend. As for him, he choked up, his tongue got thick, and he could not remember anything he wanted to say.

Chuck changed the subject abruptly. "I didn't expect you to come around again, at least until after football season."

Doug's gaze met his, and he spoke evenly. "We're not out for football anymore."

Chuck pretended to be surprised. "What's the matter? Didn't you find playing with Northwest challenging enough for guys of your ability?"

"It wasn't that." Del leaned back, crossing his legs, getting comfortable. He seethed inwardly, but he could not let Chuck know how his ridicule tore at him. "I'll let you in on a little secret. We're just too good for Northwest. Mr. Knight said he'd like to have us playing for him, but he was afraid our skill would make everyone else so jealous, it would tear down the team's morale. We couldn't have that, now, could we?"

Chuck seemed disturbed by the fact that the Davis boys showed no annoyance at being dropped from the squad or at being taunted. "What happened?" he persisted, as though he did not already know. "Did you get kicked off the team?"

"You might say that." For the first time, Doug showed irritation, and Chuck answered with a grin. He *was* bugging them a little, after all. He had begun to think he was not bothering them at all.

"Weren't you good enough?" He turned to Doug. "Is that the reason you got the boot?"

"You heard what Del said, didn't you?" Doug asked him, fighting to keep from lashing back at his antagonist.

"You got cut from the squad because you weren't good enough. That's it, isn't it?"

"Is there anything wrong with that?" the Davis boy asked.

"I guess not, but you sure haven't got much pride. That's all I can say. You must not care what people say about you." He laughed again derisively. "Most guys get real upset when Knight dumps 'em."

"Well, don't worry, Chuck; we had the whole normal set of feelings too."

Del glanced at his brother. It was as though Doug had let a curtain slip to let him peer inside. He saw for the first time how bad Doug felt about not getting to play football. He felt as bad as Del had.

"Don't you hate Knight because you got dropped?"

"No, we don't." Doug spoke first. "We both felt bad about it. But when a guy does the best he can, there's nothing else he can do, and that's no reason to hate anybody."

Chuck had no reply for that. The Davises sensed it and breathed easier.

"But," Del said, grinning, "after we got to thinking about it, we decided not playing football will give us more time to learn to ski."

"I wish I were out of here." Chuck smiled ruefully. "I'd teach you both how to ski."

"That'd be great."

Chuck was enjoying himself for the first time since they came to see him. "I could teach you a lot of things."

Several times after that, Del and Doug tried to turn the conversation with Chuck back to the fact that Jesus Christ was interested in his life. He knew what they wanted to do and steered the conversation to safer subjects, like skiing.

When visiting hours were over and they finally had to leave, they were both upset by their failure.

"Well, that was a wipeout," Doug said. "We sure didn't get very far."

"We tried," Del answered, "but he wouldn't let us. And we couldn't force him to. That wouldn't be any good."

Doug thought about that as they drove home. Del had tried to talk to Chuck about his faith, but he had not. Once or twice, he tried to say something, but his words did not come out the way he wanted them to. He failed miserably.

Doug had not failed Scot, although that was his first thought. He had actually failed God. That made it seem even worse. He wanted to see Chuck come to Christ, but he knew he did not love him enough to do a lot of praying for him. That was the real problem. That night in his private devotions, Doug spent a long while on his knees asking God to help him have the love for Chuck he ought to have.

* * *

The Davis boys went out on the slopes every chance they got in a desperate attempt to learn to ski, but they still did not know much more about the sport than they did before they started.

"I think you'd better take that book of yours back and make them give you what you paid for it," Del said. "I don't think it's a bit of good."

"I'm not giving up on it yet."

Danny came into the family room, where they were talking. "I thought you guys would be working toward the National Ski Patrol by this time."

"We would be if that book of Doug's was any good," Del said. "If we don't learn before long, I think I'm going to get my own book."

"Any more remarks out of you," his brother jibed, "and you'll just have to." In spite of the serious set to his jaw, his eyes were dancing. "I'm not going to have you making fun of my book anymore."

Danny sat down and picked up a book. "Maybe you'd better go up and take a few lessons until you've learned the fundamentals."

"We thought of that. The only trouble is that lessons cost money, and that happens to be one thing we don't have too much of," Doug replied.

"That's when Doug had this marvelous idea," Del broke in. "He bought this book that's supposed to give us all the shortcuts about how to ski."

"It came highly recommended to me, I'll have you know."

"By your worst enemy."

"Okay. Okay." He shrugged his exasperation. "If that's the way it is, we'll just throw the book away."

"I wouldn't have you do that for anything," his brother persisted. "It's good for a lot of laughs."

"Come off it." Doug's irritation was slight but unmistakable. "You know we've both learned a lot from that book."

"We sure have. We learned that 'skiing is exuberance.' Did you know that, Danny?"

The youthful flying instructor had difficulty keeping the mirth from his eyes. "I can't say that I did."

"And that's not all. We learned that football players *never* have trouble learning to ski. I guess that shows the coach knew what he was doing when he kicked us off the squad. We've sure had plenty of trouble trying to get a little skill."

Doug's nose wrinkled distastefully. "Okay, wise guy! The next time, I won't even let you look at my book. Now, what do you think of that?"

"Don't say it! You're breaking my heart!" Del wiped imaginary tears from his eyes.

"You can clown around about it now, but I'll be skiing like a pro, and you'll still be on the beginner's slope with the little kids. And it'll all be because you made so much fun of my book I wouldn't let you read any more out of it. Then you'll be sorry."

Del and Doug had a lot of fun kidding about their first clumsy attempts to learn to ski, but the only other person outside the family that they had mentioned it to was Chuck Grover. They were surprised a couple of days later when several guys asked them to have lunch with them at noon and the subject came up. Kurt Nordland, the mayor's son, seemed surprised that they did not know how to ski.

"You're kidding, aren't you?" he asked.

"It sounds stupid, I know," Del agreed, "but we're sure working on it. We'll learn how if it kills us."

Doug was afraid his brother would mention the instruction book. He caught Del's gaze with his own, and that warned him to silence. "We're getting there. It may take us a little time, but we'll make it."

"Doesn't *anybody* ski in Minnesota?" another boy asked.

"Sure," Del countered. "Everybody but Doug and me."

"Seriously," Doug said, "there aren't any hills to speak of around Fairview. I guess that's the reason we've never learned before."

Kurt's expression changed, as though a new thought just occurred to him. "Hey, I've got a great idea. My dad's got a cabin up on the ridge above town. Why don't we go up there and stay Friday night? Saturday I'll teach you to ski. Okay?"

Del and Doug looked at one another. They had heard what a great guy Kurt was on the slats. They heard it said that if Northwest had a ski team, Kurt would be the captain. He had money enough to go to the better runs, and he had taken a lot of professional instruction. Where most of the guys had to pick up the finer points of skiing from each other, if they learned them at all, Kurt had the best instructor available in Colorado. He bragged that he could go over to Aspen any time he wanted to, but everybody thought he exaggerated a little about that.

"What do you say?" he asked when Del and Doug did not answer immediately.

"We'll let you know." They did not tell him that they had to check out such things with Danny. Kurt would never understand that and would only laugh at them. Checking with Danny and Kay did not bother them too much; they did not mind having to clear such things with their foster parents. But they hated with a passion being taunted about it.

CHAPTER 4

THAT WAS A CLOSE SHAVE!

When Danny came home that evening, the boys asked him about going up to the Nordland cabin the next weekend. He did not give them his answer immediately. He wanted to know something about Kurt Nordland and asked if anyone else was going to be there. The boys told him they thought there would just be the three of them.

"At least he didn't say anything about it if he plans to have anyone else there," Doug said.

"I'm sure it'll be just the three of us. He said we'd spend Saturday learning to ski."

Danny and Kay left the final decision with the boys but told them they did think it would be a good chance for them to learn to ski. Del and Doug were glad for the opportunity to have someone teach them to ski, but the offer vaguely disturbed Doug.

"We've never been around Kurt at all, Del," he

said. "In fact, we hardly knew him before today. Why would he come up to us and offer to take us up to his dad's cabin and teach us to ski? It doesn't make sense."

"Maybe he heard about that stupid book of yours and felt sorry for us."

"Okay. Okay." Doug changed the subject. He was probably being silly, getting upset by a little thing like that, he told himself. He guessed they ought to be glad for a chance to have an instructor for free.

Kurt seemed glad when the boys told him they would like to go up to his dad's cabin with him Friday evening after school.

"That's great." His smile stretched broadly across his lean, Scandinavian face. "That'll give me time enough to get everything lined up."

"What do you mean?" Doug asked suspiciously. "There isn't anything to line up for an overnight for three guys in a cabin, is there?"

"Sure there is. I'll have to buy some food and chop some wood for the fireplace. And I want to wax my skis. Say, I'm buying a new jacket. Either of you want to buy my old one?"

Doug filled Kurt in on what Minnesota winters were like.

Kurt then insisted that the Davis boys go up to the cabin in his car with him as soon as school was out Friday afternoon. For a while, that was the arrangement. At the last minute, however, they had to make a change.

"We'll have to get up there on our own," Del said when they saw Kurt at lunch. "We can't get away until after dinner tonight."

Kurt made no effort to hide his disappointment. "How come?"

"Danny's got some heavy work to do at the airport," Doug explained. "I think he's taking the engine out of a plane or something, and he wants us to give him a hand."

"Can't it wait?"

"Not a chance. But you go ahead, and we'll come up right after dinner."

Kurt continued to insist that they join him right after school, letting Danny's work go until they returned. When he was unsuccessful, he muttered angrily under his breath. "Well, it's too late to change things now. I'll have to go on up to the cabin as soon as school's out. You can get up there some way, can't you?"

"Oh, sure," Doug replied, "Danny'll let us use the car."

"There's one more thing I almost forgot to tell you." Sarcasm tainted Kurt's voice. "There's no way to call from the cabin, so you won't be able to call Danny when you get there and tell him that you made it. He'll have to wait till Saturday to find out if you're all right."

Doug flinched. "I think he can stand it."

"That's fine. We sure wouldn't want him to be upset, would we?"

Doug began to wish they had refused Kurt's invitation. He had no real reason for feeling that way except that it made him furious to have anyone ridicule Danny or Kay. He wanted to defend them heatedly, but he realized that would not do any good. It would just make Kurt louder and more sarcastic than ever.

When the Davis boys reached the airport after school, Danny was not quite ready to have them help him. They had to wait half an hour before they could even start to work. And, even with the help of a hoist, getting the engine out took longer than either they or Danny had expected. It was dark and after six o'clock by the time they had finished and put the tools away.

Del and Doug ate as quickly as possible after they got home, lashed their skis to the top of the car, and made their way out of Rock Point in the direction of the mountains.

"Are you sure we're on the right road?" Del asked.

"I'm sure of it," he said; "but to tell you the truth, I don't care very much."

Doug shrugged indifferently. He did not even recheck the map.

They were a quarter of a mile from the cabin when they first heard the wild, syncopated beat of the drum.

Del slowed, instinctively. "What's that?" he demanded.

"Sounds like music to me."

"He's sure got it turned up; that's all I can say."

They listened again intently.

"You don't suppose Kurt planned a party for tonight, do you?" Doug asked uneasily.

"Could be."

"He wouldn't do that, though," Doug said. "We're coming up here to ski."

"If it is a party, we'll get out of here, but quick. I don't want to have anything more to do with his kind of parties than I have to."

They continued to drive up the narrow, twisting trail. The closer they got, the louder the beat of the drums became. They had not gone far, when the sound of the guitar filled in around the beat to provide an accompaniment for the soloist, a girl who sounded like she was wailing more than singing.

"I don't think that's recorded," Doug said thoughtfully. He did not know why he thought that; he had no firm basis for it.

"Well," Del said, "we'll soon know. I saw the lights through the trees as we turned just now."

One final turn, and there was the Nordland cabin, ablaze with lights. Half a dozen cars were pulled up in a row in front of it.

"It is a party!" Doug exclaimed. "Let's get out of here!"

"We have to go up far enough to turn around." Del's fear rose quickly. He did not know why, but he felt as though they had to get out of there as quickly as possible. He was in the process of turning when

Kurt came outside, a girl slightly younger than he following him.

"I see you finally got here," he called out, his voice booming over the still, winter air. "Come on in! The party's just gettin' good."

Doug put down the window. "No, thanks."

"You don't know what you're missing." He looked at the girl.

Del and Doug glanced quickly at each other. They knew they did not want to go inside, but with Kurt insisting, they were suddenly hesitant.

"What do you think?" Doug spoke guardedly so they would not be overheard.

"I don't want to go in there."

"Neither do I. I just happened to think, though, that it might be a chance for us to show him and the others that we're not boring and old-fashioned. It could give us a good chance to witness to them."

Del felt the same pull to join the kids inside, despite his protests. It was no fun being laughed at. That had not happened yet; but it would, as soon as Kurt and the others saw they were not going to come in. He could not quite see the witnessing bit, though. How could a guy talk to anyone about Jesus Christ in a place like that? On the other hand, if they did go in, it would show Kurt and whoever else was there that they were not afraid to go into a place where the kids were doing things they disapproved of. It might show them all how different he and Doug were. They would see it when they did not dance or drink. Maybe there was someone inside who was too weak to keep from doing the things everybody else did. They might be able to help give that person the courage to do what was right. When he thought about it that way, Del could make a good case for going in. Besides, the beat of the music was tugging at him.

While they were reasoning with themselves, Kurt pulled the door shut to close out some of the booming music behind him. "Come on," he called. "We're not gonna hurt you."

Doug was weakening as much as Del was. "What do you think?"

"Come on in!" Kurt cried. "And let us get you started. If that happens a couple of times, you'll find out where it's at, and you won't be such sissies."

The boys opened their car doors and started to climb out. The boy on the porch could not keep back his grin. "Now, that's more like it." He came down off the steps and sauntered slowly in the direction of the car, the girl tagging after him, pulling at his arm. He jerked away in disgust. "Leave me alone, will ya?"

"But you *promised*." Her voice had a strange, haunting, drawn-out quality, as though the cold air suspended it endlessly.

"I'll get it for you in a minute."

"That's what you keep telling me, but I've got to have it right now. I'm all strung out."

"I'll get it for you. Come on in, guys, so I can take care of Snooksie and get her off my back."

She tugged at his arm again.

"You don't need any more." He seemed embarrassed. "You're stoned already!"

Her laugh chilled Doug and Del.

Del and Doug got the same message from the weird acting girl who tagged after Kurt. They reacted almost simultaneously, scrambling back into the car and slamming the doors.

Kurt realized what was happening and grabbed her by the arm, swearing loudly. "Get back in the house, Snooksie! You'll blow everything!" He dragged her back onto the porch.

"Come on, Del!" Doug cried. "Let's get out of here!"

The boy on the porch gave Snooksie a quick shove toward the door with a profane order to go inside and stay there. Then he dashed to the car. "Wait a minute, guys! Don't go! It's not what you think!"

Del started the engine and shifted into drive.

Kurt was shouting that the kids had decided to put on a little act for Del and Doug to get them upset. "Don't leave now! The party's just gettin' good!"

By this time, the kids at the party realized something was going on outside, and a few shouldered out the door.

"Get with it!" Doug cried. "They might try to stop us!"

Del, too, sensed what was about to happen and

jammed the accelerator against the floorboard as half a dozen guys surged down the steps and through the snow toward the car. The cleated tires bit into the crusted snow and threw chunks of it in the faces of those who were closest. Their cursing and threats followed Del and Doug down the narrow lane.

"We've got it made!" Del murmured, fear still tightening his throat.

"Yeah, if you don't drive so fast we slip off the road."

The driver glanced in the rearview mirror. "I just don't want them to get in their cars and try to follow us."

"You don't think they'd be stupid enough to do that?"

"Who knows what they'd do?"

By this time, a sort of delayed reaction set in, and the boys began shaking. Doug wiped the sweat from his face. "What is going on back there, Del, a weed party?"

"My guess is that it's more than that."

"We should've known there was something fishy when Kurt offered to have us up here to teach us to ski. He doesn't act like the kind of guy who'd want to do anything for anybody."

"And we were almost crazy enough to fall for it."

They drove out to the main road before either spoke again.

CHAPTER 5

ONLY THE BEGINNING

"You know, Doug, we both were pretty stupid back there."

"That's just what I was thinking."

"When you asked me to go in," Del continued, "I started arguing with myself. And, believe me, I found some great reasons why we ought to stay for the party. I didn't want to go in and do what the other guys were doing, but I didn't like the idea of being laughed at. I wanted to prove to them that we're all right. I wanted them to know we could be anywhere they were."

Doug nodded. "Me, too," he added. "And I'd just about convinced myself that we should go in."

"And if we had, you know what would've happened."

"They wouldn't have any respect for us, especially not Chuck Grover. We wouldn't be able to get anywhere with witnessing to him if we had gone to the party."

For a time, they discussed Chuck as they drove home. Doug recalled a devotional time at home when Danny had talked about the same subject. He had told them that God was interested, first, in what they were, and that He wanted them to be clean before Him. Then He wanted them to serve Him as clean vessels. Danny had even mentioned that they should be careful of the sort of places they went and the kind of people they associated with because it was too easy to try something "once" or to be carried away with what the group wanted to do.

"I guess that would take care of our going into Kurt's cabin tonight, wouldn't it?" Del asked.

Doug agreed with him.

They talked about going home right away but decided to stop at the nearest cafe first. They both could use a good warm cup of cocoa.

Del turned in at an all-night truck stop.

"Doesn't look too inviting," Doug remarked, seeing the run-down restaurant with its neon sign only half lit up.

"You like Kurt's place better?" Del asked. Laughing, the brothers headed for the shabby cafe.

Shortly after ten o'clock, the boys reached home and went inside. Danny and Kay heard them at the back door and rushed to the kitchen.

"Oh, it's you!" Relief was evident in Danny's voice.

"Sure it's us. Who'd you expect?"

"We thought you were at Kurt Nordland's party," Kay said.

"It looked a little rough for us, so we didn't stay."

Doug's eyes rounded. "How did you know about the party?"

"It's been on the news twice this evening. The authorities raided it, and they've got a bunch of kids in jail."

The boys gasped.

"Raided it? What for?"

"We don't know the whole story," Kay continued. "We were so concerned about you both that Danny called the station to see if you were there. The officer in charge wouldn't tell him anything except that you hadn't been brought in with the others."

"He asked me to call him if you did come home," Danny said. "They want to talk to you."

"But why?" Del asked, his voice a bit too loud. Their fear rushed back.

"We don't know anything about the party or what went on there," Doug protested. "We didn't even get all the way out of the car."

"That's right. We almost went in but changed our minds and split when we didn't like the looks of what was going on."

Danny called the station. In a moment he was back. "They want us to come down to the station tonight or in the morning. They want to ask you a few questions."

"What'll we tell them?"

"Just what you've told me – the truth."

The boys decided to go down to the station that night.

"I don't think I'd be able to sleep if I knew we had to do that tomorrow," Doug said.

"Me either. I'd just as soon go down and get it over with."

Danny went to the police station with them to talk to the officer in charge. The sergeant asked them about the plans for the party and if they knew what other kids were going to be there. They wanted to know how long they had been friends of Kurt and the other guys.

"We really just got acquainted with Kurt this week," Del said. "We got to talking to him, and he invited us up to the cabin to ski."

"We don't know whether we're friends of anyone else who was there. We didn't recognize the cars outside, and we don't know who was in the cabin," Doug added.

The questioning went much better than they thought it would. The officer came back to several points asking them for a little more information; but he was courteous and seemed to believe them. At last he indicated he had nothing more to ask about.

"I'll have the statement typed up in the morning, and you can stop by in the afternoon and sign it."

Del seemed surprised that there was nothing more they would have to do. "Is–is that all you want of us?"

The officer looked up, quickly, nailing him with a stare. "Is there anything else you have to tell us?"

"Oh, no. No. I just thought–" his voice trailed away.

The silence was long and painful.

"If you think of anything else that might help us, come in or give us a call, will you?"

A moment later, they were outside and on their way to the car.

"I'm sure glad that's over," Del said.

"Me, too." Doug turned to his brother. "What was the matter with you in there just now? I thought you were going to fool around and get yourself locked up."

"I was beginning to think so too. All I meant was that I was surprised that he didn't ask us a lot more questions and be a lot more suspicious about our answers. He seemed to believe what we told him."

Danny drove home. He too was noticeably more relaxed. "I didn't tell you about the other news I heard, did I? They said the police have been watching the Nordland cabin for some time. They've heard reports about the kind of parties Kurt's been throwing. If that's the case, and I'm sure it is, they probably know who's been coming to those parties. They may even have been watching the cabin when you guys drove up and then left right away."

Del sighed audibly. He and Doug had almost gone into the cabin telling themselves they could be testimonies by being there without taking part in what was going on. That had been close! If they had gone in there, they would be in jail right now. The cops would never have bought that "testimony" bit. He guessed God was really taking care of them.

* * *

Northwest High was large and more impersonal than some schools, but the police raid on the Nordland mountain cabin caused a lot of excitement, especially among those who knew Kurt and the others. When Doug and Del walked into school the next Monday morning, four or five guys were huddled together just inside the main door, their voices low and guarded. One of them squinted in Doug's direction, beckoning him to join them with an almost imperceptible jerk of the head. Del would have gone on, but Doug grasped his wrist and pulled him back.

"Hi."

"That was somethin' about the cops bustin' Kurt, wasn't it?" a guy named Stein asked pointedly.

The Davis boys nodded.

"I never thought it'd happen," another boy put in.

"Neither did I. It was bad. They caught him with weed and acid and speed – the whole bit. And that stupid chick of his was as high as Pike's Peak when the cops got there."

"I don't know what he sees in her," the other boy said. "She's freaked out half the time."

"She'll get a chance to turn off now, but good," one of the others put in. "They were still locked up this morning, all nine of them."

"Imagine that!" Stein exclaimed. "And Kurt's old man is the mayor. I didn't think anyone'd *dare* lay a hand on him!"

"I still think they've got him down there to make it look good. They won't do anything to him."

"Just the same, I'm glad I wasn't up there. They asked me, but my old man took my wheels away last week, and I couldn't get a ride. Was I ever lucky."

Stein had stopped listening to the conversation by this time. His gaze was fixed coldly on Del and Doug. "How come you guys split before the cops showed?"

"They were just smart," somebody else answered. "They were smart or lucky, one."

"I wasn't asking you!" An accusing tone crept into Stein's voice as he continued. "You both were supposed to be up there, weren't you?"

"That's right." Doug didn't know why he felt so defensive. "You heard Kurt ask us to go skiing. We didn't even *know* there was going to be a party."

"Oh, come off it! You might make the cops believe that stuff, but not Ernie Stein. Every guy in school knew about those parties of Kurt's. Don't act so innocent."

"Doug's telling you the truth," Del broke in. "We probably would have been up there when the cops came, but we happened to arrive a little late, and the party had already started when we got there. When we saw the kind of a party it was, we split."

Stein pushed closer to him belligerently. "What'd you do then? Go to the cops?"

"Cool it, Stein!" one of the others said. "I know Kurt's your best friend, but you know that whole bunch has been askin' for trouble. They've been havin' those parties just about every week since last spring."

"Sure, but *this* is the week they got busted, and it's the first time these two were invited. I don't know what that says to you, but I know what it says to me! And I don't like it."

"Be reasonable. They didn't have to have anyone tell on them. Like you said, practically everybody in school knew about those parties." The others nodded in assent.

Del and Doug appreciated their defender, a guy they had never met.

Stein sat up straight slowly, doubt still clouding his coarse features. It was obvious that he was not ready to accept the fact that Del and Doug had not caused his friend's difficulties.

"I'm warnin' you both right now," he muttered darkly, "if anyone puts the finger on Kurt Nordland, he's goin' to have to answer to me." He leaned forward until his face was inches away from Doug's. "Understand?"

"Perfectly," Doug answered calmly, the fear and defensiveness gone. "We didn't go to the cops about that party last night. But you might as well know it now. If we'd known for sure what kind of a party it was, we probably would have gone straight to the police station."

One of the guys gasped. Nobody around Northwest stood up to Stein that way – and got away with it.

Anger drove the color from Stein's broad cheeks, and he clenched his fists belligerently. "You'd rat on them?" He couldn't believe it. "You mean, you've got guts enough to stand there and tell me to my face that you'd squeal?"

"You can call it anything you like, but kids who're fooling around with drugs ought to be turned in. It'd be a favor to them, and it would sure be a favor to the other kids in school."

The burly senior acted as though he was about to slug the Davis boy right in the hall. "What do you mean?"

"They're not satisfied with ruining themselves. They've got to get as many new kids turned on to drugs as they can. They ought to be stopped."

"I've got a notion to let you have it right here! You ugly little snitch!" Stein's big fist started forward, but he was able to get control of himself.

Del pushed forward to stand beside his brother. "If that's the name of the game, you've got two of us to take care of!"

"And don't think I can't do it! You guys talk big, but wait until I get through with you. You'll wish you'd kept your big fat mouths shut."

Fear tingled Del's spine, but as Stein blustered, he began to relax. He saw something in the big senior's face that he had not noticed before.

"Come on, Doug." He touched his brother's arm. "It's stupid for guys our age to stand here like four-year-olds working ourselves up for a tantrum." There was no fear in his manner. "We're a little too old for that."

The others laughed, and Stein turned almost purple. He cocked his fist once more and brought it forward several inches so Del could not avoid noticing it. "Call *me* a kid, will you? I don't have to take that kind of guff off of anybody."

They started away.

"You come back here! I ain't through talkin' to you yet."

"Cool it, Stein," Del said mildly. "We all know you're a big boy."

He was still muttering profane threats as the Davis boys left him and casually walked away. The group broke up with that, and the guy who first defended Del and Doug walked with them in the direction of their lockers.

"I'm Henry Warren." A smile split his freckled face. "Call me Hank."

Del and Doug introduced themselves.

"I really got a bang out of the way you handled Ernie Stein. You won't have to worry about him. He'll leave you alone."

"I sort of figured he was bluffing," Del responded.

"Ol' Stein doesn't mind getting in a fight once in a while, but he's not going to tackle anything like an even chance. He's too afraid of getting hurt."

Doug grinned. "I'm glad to know that. I was beginning to think we'd have to find a bodyguard."

"You don't have to worry about Stein jumping you, but–" Hank's expression changed.

"But, what?" The tone in their new friend's voice was disturbing. "You act as though there's something else we should know about Stein," Doug said.

"There is." He was speaking little above a whisper. "Ernie isn't the kind of a guy I'd choose for an enemy. I'll tell you that much."

"How come?"

"He's clever and sneaky. He might be scared to back up all his fight talk, but he'll do something underhanded to get back at you. You can count on it."

"Thanks. We'll keep our eyes open," Del said.

"He's a good friend of Kurt Nordland's, and he means it when he says he'll get back at anybody who does anything to Kurt."

They talked for a minute or two, and Hank started

toward his own locker, telling them he would see them around. Doug brought him back with a question.

"There's one more thing I just happened to think of. Is Ernie a good friend of a guy named Chuck Grover too?"

Hank's facial muscles tightened. "What makes you ask that?"

"Something I just thought of."

"As a matter of fact, yes. Kurt and Ernie and Chuck are together just about all the time. Chuck's in the hospital, I understand. Kurt and Ernie probably go up there every night."

Doug nodded thoughtfully. That explained a lot of things.

CHAPTER 6

A WHOLE NEW WORLD
FOR DOUG

Doug had admired Tina Nicholson since that time last summer when he first met her at Chuck's uncle's ranch, but he had not allowed himself to think about the possibility of getting better acquainted with her. He certainly had not figured on sitting with her at lunch that noon. It just happened.

Del had left his fourth hour textbook in his locker and went to get it, leaving Doug in line alone. He thought of waiting for his brother, but changed his mind and went to find a place to sit, his tray loaded with food. He saw Tina sitting alone at a table, but he did not have the courage to sit down with her. Why would she want a guy like him around?

But she spoke warmly. "Hi, Doug."

He stopped beside her, wishing he could think of

something bright and witty to say. He never could come up with anything when he really wanted to.

He looked blankly at her, hoping she did not notice how nervous he was.

"Is this seat taken?" he asked hesitantly.

"Not until now."

He pulled out a chair and sat down. "I'm glad Del forgot to pick up his chemistry book."

Her eyes widened with curiosity, and he realized she didn't have a clue as to what he was talking about.

"I mean that's the reason I'm alone," he tried to explain. Then he realized how silly that sounded, as though he could not have left Del on his own and come over to sit with her. "I mean – oh, skip it."

Her smile graciously pushed aside his uneasiness. "I'm glad you came over to sit with me."

His eyelids widened. He believed she meant it. She actually meant it! It made him weak to realize that she wanted to talk to him. "So am I."

That sounded dopey too. He could have kicked himself for being so stupid. If she were one of DeeDee's friends who had come to visit, or even if one were sitting with him in the school lunchroom, he would not have had any difficulty talking to her. He would be teasing her about a boyfriend, talking about the last football game or the difficulties they had had the summer before working at the dude ranch. He had never had any problem talking to girls until a couple of minutes ago. But trying to carry on a conversation with Tina was different, and he did not know why. His throat choked, and his eyes got glassy just thinking about it. He knew he had never even seen a girl half as pretty as she was. And he was having lunch with her!

She was sitting there quietly, toying with her fork. And he knew why. She was waiting for him to say something, and was probably wondering why she had encouraged such an idiot to eat lunch with her. When he finally got up nerve enough to say something, she spoke at the same time. They both laughed nervously.

"I'm sorry, Doug. What were you going to say?"

"It didn't amount to anything." The truth was, he could not remember. "What were you going to say?"

"You tell me first."

He eyed her questioningly and was about to repeat his protest, but stopped. If they kept that up, they would not say anything during the whole meal.

"Know something?" He grinned sheepishly. "This is ridiculous."

That broke the tension, and they both laughed. They were still laughing when Del came up.

"Hi." He was grinning at his brother. "What's so funny?"

"You wouldn't understand."

"Try me. I'm a very understanding guy."

Doug scowled at him.

Del tried to sound disturbed. "I'll go," he said, "but

I want you to know I'm crushed. My own brother doesn't want me around."

"You can sit down," Tina broke in. "There's another chair here."

But Doug's eyes warned him away. He knew that look meant, "Get out of here or I'll pulverize you!" He really did not want to sit with them; he just wanted to needle that brother of his.

"Doug's hurt me now," he said, turning. "I know enough to take a hint. I won't stay where I'm not wanted."

"Nobody's hinting," Doug retorted darkly. "I'm telling you."

He knew Del would be on his back about Tina Nicholson as soon as they were alone, and he waited expectantly for the blow to fall. However, his brother said nothing at all to him about her when they changed classes or went home together. He did not mention anything about her until they were all sitting at the dinner table that evening.

"I've got a question I'd like to ask you, Danny." His face was serious.

Doug's gaze came up quickly. He knew Del as well as he knew himself. This was it. He braced himself, cheeks coloring.

"Sure, go ahead."

"Wouldn't you say brothers are supposed to be nice to each other – and especially triplet brothers?"

Danny's gaze met Doug's curiously. "I'd have to say so."

"You wouldn't say it was nice for one brother to tell another brother to get lost and go eat his lunch all alone, would you?"

"Lay off," Doug muttered under his breath.

"And especially when there was an empty place at the table right beside him. I wouldn't think that was very nice, would you?"

"It wasn't like that at all," his brother mumbled.

"That's not all. The other person who was sitting at the table with this brother asked the lonely brother to sit down and eat with them so he could join in on the stimulating conversation and not be lonely anymore. But the one brother wouldn't let him. He chased him away. And I don't call that very nice. Would you, Danny?"

DeeDee came quickly to Doug's defense. "I couldn't see anything wrong with Doug's insisting that you eat alone. Under the circumstances, I think you were way off base."

Doug glared at her. DeeDee might think she was helping, but she was not. She was just making things worse. There was no use for him to try to explain. He knew that Del was just trying to get him going.

"Then there were 'circumstances'?" Danny was enjoying it as much as Del.

"I'll say there were circumstances. You should have seen them. Long blond hair and dreamy blue eyes and a beautiful car in the driveway. You said it, Danny. There were circumstances."

"You're just jealous, that's all," DeeDee continued. "I wish certain people in this house would *grow up*." She stared down at her plate.

"Then you saw him too!" Del exclaimed triumphantly.

"There wasn't anything to see. How many times do I have to tell you that?"

"There's part of the story I'm not getting," Danny said, trying to be serious. "Just who was this who happened to be sitting with Doug?"

"Little Miss Cadillac. And you should've seen them, Danny. They were sitting there laughing like a couple of refugees from a psycho ward. They didn't even talk to each other. They just sat there and giggled."

"And who's Little Miss Cadillac? That's what I want to know."

"She's the girl who lives next door. She's been flirting with Doug with those big, soft blue eyes ever since we moved in."

"Do you mean Tina Nicholson?" Kay asked.

"That's right." DeeDee was indignant. "Del's hysterical because Doug had lunch with Tina this noon. She's a nice Christian girl, and I think it's nice that they ate together."

"So does Doug. That's what I've been trying to tell you."

"And what if he does like her?" DeeDee persisted. "What's so terrible about that?"

"Do you think he'll be able to take her out in our beat up old set of wheels, Danny? It sure won't be the same as those Cadillacs she's used to."

"We're not going to buy a new car for him to take her out. I can tell you both that, right now. So if she goes out with him, I guess they'll have to walk or put up with our car."

Doug pushed back from the table. "You people make me tired!" he exploded. "All I did was have lunch with a girl! Now you've got me dating her. We're just friends. That's *all*."

"Give him time, Danny. Give him time. You should have seen that goony look in his eyes when he sat across from her. Doug's flipped out this time. He's really gone. He'll never be the same again."

"Okay, you guys. If it'll make you happy, have your fun."

He pulled his chair back up to the table and continued eating. There were a lot worse girls they could be teasing him about, he decided. At least she was cuter than most.

Doug had not actually thought about having a date with Tina, but going out with her might not be so bad. In fact, now that he considered it, it sounded like a great idea. She had a good sense of humor, and she was easily the prettiest girl in the whole school.

As far as he was concerned, she was the prettiest girl in Rock Point. Being with her could be a lot of fun.

Only she probably would not want to go out with him after he made such a mess of everything at noon. He might just as well forget Tina. She would pick a guy who was smarter and more exciting to be with than he was if she wanted to date someone.

Surprisingly, he was disturbed by that. And he had not thought he would be.

After supper, Danny said to Doug on the side, "Hope we didn't go too far tonight. I've met Tina's dad, and he's a good man; so I'm sure Tina's nice too. Don't be afraid to get to know her better or bring her over. If Del doesn't leave you alone, I'll have a man-to-man talk with him."

Doug smiled. *Why couldn't Del be like that?* he wondered.

CHAPTER 7

STORM CLOUDS RISING

The rest of the week it seemed to Del and Doug that the kids at school could talk of little else than what had happened to Kurt Nordland and his friends at the party. They had all been taken before the judge on Monday and released on bond.

The stories that were out were wild, and nobody knew for sure what was truth and what was exaggeration. The fact that Del and Doug came close to being involved was widely known in the junior class and caused the kids to come to them for verification of each new tale.

Kurt was supposed to be a pusher, according to one account, who was getting his merchandise directly from a Denver connection who dealt with the Syndicate. Another story had him smoking a little weed once in a while but leaving the other stuff alone. Or he was supposed to have bought a little weed but did not do any pushing. Still another claimed he did not use *any* kind of drugs and was framed by some unknown person or persons.

Some of the kids thought Del and Doug had something to do with it. No one accused them directly. It was a more subtle thing that the Davis boys sensed rather than heard openly. They talked about it when they were alone, but did not say anything to anyone else, not even DeeDee or Danny and Kay.

"Maybe it's just our imaginations," Doug observed as they were driving to their private ski resort.

Del could not agree with that. "No, some of the guys think we actually were in on it and were lucky enough to split before the cops got there."

"As long as the police don't think we were in on it," Doug said, "that's all I care."

"I'm beginning to wonder if anything'll happen to them. They're all back in school now, the same as before. And they sure don't act any different than they did before."

The next day as the Davis boys approached the school building, they saw Chuck Grover swinging awkwardly out of his mother's car and opening the back door to get his crutches.

"There's Chuck." Doug turned and approached him. "Hi. Can we give you a hand?"

He scowled harshly. "I'll manage."

"Let me carry those books for you."

"I told you I'd manage!" He got his books and started slowly up on the sidewalk.

"When did you get out of the hospital?" Del asked.

Chuck stopped halfway to the door and faced him. "That's none of your business!" He swore at him. "Any guys who rat on my buddies are no friends of mine!"

With that, he went on to the building, where someone else came and helped him with his books.

"He hasn't changed a bit," Del said. "And Scot thinks *we* can get through to him."

"I've seen friendlier guys in my time."

"Me, too." Del fell silent until they were at their lockers. "You know, Chuck bothers me," he said.

"What brings that on?"

"You remember what Hank Warren told us about him? He's a good friend of Kurt Nordland and Ernie Stein. I just wonder if he's going to try to get back at us."

"Hank was warning us about Ernie," Doug reminded him.

"I know, but Chuck's the one who's got the most reason to be down on you and me. We blew the whistle on him for giving DeeDee a bad time, and he apparently blames us because he fell and broke his leg."

"We didn't have anything to do with that. In fact, we are the ones who found him and got help."

"I know that, but a guy like him probably blames us for making him get uptight enough to run away. He must've set it up with Kurt to invite us to that party in the first place. And when the whole gang was arrested and we weren't, he could be blaming us for that too."

Doug shuddered. "You know, Chuck is one guy I'm afraid of. There's no knowing what he might do."

That same chilling apprehension weighed on them all day. Chuck did not say any more to them when they met him in the halls or the lunchroom, but he seemed to hate them passionately.

As the undefeated football season neared the end, the basketball coach announced that practice was to begin the first of the following week. Doug decided immediately that he was going to try out for the team. Del insisted that he never would. They had a long talk that night as they lay in their beds.

"There's no use in my going out," he told his brother. "It'll probably be the football squad all over again, only quicker."

"I don't think so. From what I hear, they really need guys for basketball. They graduated most of the squad last year. The coach is scrounging for guys who can do him some good."

"That lets me out." Del's smile came and went.

"How do you know till you've tried? You can run, and you're quick. You ought to make a good basketball player."

Del had to think about that. He could not say that he had enjoyed the game when he played it back in Fairview, but that had been a long while ago. He had matured a lot since then. He was several inches taller, for one thing, and had a couple of years of experience playing football. He might be able to handle himself on the basketball court.

He turned his attention to his brother, suspiciously. "How come you're so fired up about basketball all of a sudden?"

"I always have been."

"Oh, now, don't give me that. I suppose Tina wants you to go out and make a big name for yourself so she can be proud of you."

"She doesn't have a thing to do with it."

"I don't suppose you ever discussed the subject with her. It never even came up, eh?"

"That's no concern of yours."

"I know it. I was just making an observation."

"For your information, the subject has come up," Doug said, trying hard to explain exactly how it was. "We did talk about it when we were having lunch."

"I knew it. I knew it."

"But she didn't try to influence me one way or the other."

"Oh, sure." He scoffed at his brother good-naturedly. "Sure."

"It's the truth."

"I believe you."

"You do not. I can tell by that silly tone in your voice."

Del laughed. "The only trouble with you is that your conscience is beginning to bother you."

Del and Doug saw Chuck Grover several times that week, considering the size of the school. They also saw Ernie Stein occasionally, and on three or four occasions they saw Kurt Nordland. The muscles in his face were taut, and his eyes were dull and expressionless as he looked past them. As far as he was concerned, he did not even know them. He was usually with Ernie, and once or twice they saw him with Chuck and two or three others; but there was a difference in the way they went down the halls and talked, even to each other. The laughter vanished from their faces, and there was no longer any cockiness or swagger in the way they walked. There used to be a crowd around them wherever they went. Now, however, they seldom lingered where the other kids congregated. Del and Doug were careful to speak, but there was no response. None of the gang wanted to have anything to do with them.

After one rebuff, the boys discussed it over lunch. "I'd like to go up to Kurt and tell him how sorry we are about the whole mess," Doug said, "but I don't think he'd even listen to me."

"You're right. He doesn't want to have anything to do with us. And I think it'll be better for us if that's the way things stay."

"I suppose you're right." There was not much anyone could do to help Kurt and his friends right then unless they would listen to the gospel if it was presented to them. Doug did not know whether he had ever had much contact with the church. He knew Kurt had not been around their church since their family started going there. Of course, Rock Point had several good churches.

The next Monday, Del and Doug reported to the gym for the first basketball practice of the season. Del had been sure he was not going out for the team until the time came to go down to the locker room and sign up.

"I don't know what I'm doing this for," he mumbled. "It's just a waste of everybody's time."

"You'll be glad you did."

"How come? Has Little Miss Cadillac got a friend?" Doug glared at him.

Checking out equipment was the same as the routine at Fairview. The regulars came confidently into the locker room, got their uniforms, and started to change. The others hung back uncertainly, not sure what to do next.

The coach, Mr. Nelson, came over and talked with Del and Doug briefly, asking them about their former experience and letting them know he was glad to have them on the squad.

When he was gone, Del turned his head and spoke quietly so he could not be overheard. "I wonder how happy he'll be when he sees me play."

Doug's disgust showed through. "That's the trouble with you. You don't care enough about making the team."

The coaches had done their recruiting among the student body well, and the locker room was crowded. Out in the gym, they lined the squad up in long rows and an assistant led the boys in conditioning exercises. When that was over, they had the boys jog around the floor. Some of the guys who had never been out for a sport before were complaining about the hard work, but Del and Doug knew what to expect. It would not be long until they would be able to start doing things that were a little more fun. At the moment, getting in condition was the important thing.

After practice Del and Doug left the gym by a side door and headed for the parking lot. They had not talked with Chuck Grover since the day they had first seen him come to school after getting out of the hospital. For that reason they were surprised when he spotted them from a car, waved, and had Ernie, the driver, swing over to the curb and stop.

"Hey, come here a minute!"

They approached the car uneasily. They still could not forget the look on his face the last time he had talked with them. It was still there, they saw, as they got closer. Only this time a faint smile masked it.

"Hi, Chuck."

"How're things going?" Doug asked.

"Never been better."

"That's good," Doug said. "I suppose you'll be getting rid of those crutches before long."

Ernie snorted. "What's that to you?"

"Oh, now, don't be like that," Chuck protested. "Don't you know? Doug and Del really care what happens to me. They *pray* for me every day."

The Davis boys flushed.

"Isn't that right?" Chuck looked up, smiling.

"As a matter of fact, it is," Doug said. He found it hard to talk. "We pray that you will put your trust in Jesus and let Him have full control of your life."

"We're praying for you too, Ernie," Del added. "We're praying that you'll become a Christian."

Chuck laughed. "Did you hear that, Stein? They've got your name on their list too. You want to be careful, or they'll have you on your knees telling God what a bad boy you've been."

Stein wasn't laughing, however. He stared at Del and Doug as though he could not believe it.

"Nobody ever prayed for me before."

"Come off it, Stein!" Chuck broke in. "Don't let it get to you. If they sell you that bill of goods, you'll *never* have any fun."

"Shut your big mouth!" Stein swore heatedly. "You know nobody's getting me for anything!"

Chuck turned back to Del and Doug.

"Do you feel a lot better now that Kurt and the other guys are in trouble?"

"We didn't have anything to do with that."

"I figured you'd try to lie out of it." Chuck shoved his fingers through his thick blonde hair.

"What do you mean by that?"

"You know well enough what I mean. You got the merchandise for them and then turned them in."

At first the Davis boys did not understand what he was accusing them of. The truth came slowly.

"You can't blame us for that. We didn't have anything to do with getting the drugs for them and everyone out there knows it."

Chuck's smile was tantalizing. "Do they?"

"They sure do."

"I wouldn't want to bet on it. I've been hearing some nasty rumors around school."

Del's anger flashed. "Maybe you'd better explain what you mean by that. I don't like the implication you're making."

"I don't like the way you blew the whistle on Kurt and my buddies, either."

"You can say that again!" Stein said ominously. "We don't like it when our friends get in trouble. Y'hear?"

"It was their *own fault*," Doug said. "If they hadn't wanted to get into trouble, they shouldn't have fooled around with drugs."

Chuck's laugh was grim and humorless. "If they hadn't, you wouldn't have had so much business, would you?"

Before either Del or Doug could reply, he gestured to Stein, who drove away, squealing his tires.

CHAPTER 8

FOUL DEEDS AND FOILED

Doug and Del watched until the car Chuck Grover was riding in made its way to the corner and turned in the direction of the hills. Neither spoke until the speeding car was out of sight.

"Now, what do you make of that?" Del asked numbly.

"I think he was just trying to scare us."

Del was not so sure he agreed with Doug. He had seen the naked anger in Chuck's eyes and had caught the hatred in his voice as he accused them of peddling drugs. There was no doubt about the way the other boy felt toward them.

"If Chuck can throw the blame on us for that raid, he's sure to do it."

"But how?" Doug countered. "I know how he dislikes us, but there's no way he can make us responsible for the kids getting those drugs. We went down to the police station voluntarily and gave them our story. We don't have anything to worry about."

"I hope you're right, but I sure don't trust Chuck. He'd try anything to get back at us."

They were still discussing the matter when they got home. They were surprised to find Danny and Kay sitting in the living room waiting for them, their faces somber.

"Hey, what's up?" Doug looked from one to the other curiously. "You look like cheerleaders for an accident."

Danny hesitated before saying anything.

"What is it?" Del asked. "Is there something wrong?"

"We had a phone call from the police a few minutes ago," Del's foster father answered.

"What do they want?" Doug gasped.

"Among other things, they wanted to know if you were home so they could talk to you."

"What about?"

"It seems that a couple of the kids who were at that party of Nordland's have identified you two as the ones who got the drugs for them," Danny continued.

Del turned quickly to his brother. "What did I tell you, Doug? I knew Chuck was up to something. I could tell by that look in his eyes."

Doug directed his attention to Danny, fear choking his voice. "They can't do this to us, can they?"

he demanded. "They can't blame us for something we didn't do!"

"Nobody is blaming you for something you didn't do," Danny replied. "And especially not the police. But the charge was made, and they've got to check it out. They would have come out here and arrested you if they had all the evidence they would need to convict you. The officer who called was very considerate. He said they just want to talk to you."

The boys were not convinced, however, that talking would take care of the matter. They went over to the couch and sat down, still shaken.

"You don't suppose they'll take the word of those guys against ours, do you, Danny?" Doug asked.

He had difficulty believing it was really taking place. It was some sick character's idea of a joke. He and Del had never had anything to do with drugs, much less peddle the stuff. They saw what it was doing to some of the kids at school, and they hated it. But it was happening. And there was a chance that he and Del would not be believed. That was what made it so grim.

"If the cops were watching Nordland's cabin that night," Del said, thinking back to the Friday evening when they drove out to the party in the hope that they would learn to ski the next day, "they'd know we didn't even go into the cabin."

"Of course we don't know if they were watching," Doug reminded him. "We're only guessing about that."

The boys wanted to go directly to the police station and talk to them right away. Danny insisted on calling first, however. When he came back, he told them they would have to wait until the next morning. The officer in charge of the case had gone home and would not be on duty until the following morning.

"So I made arrangements for you to talk with him tomorrow morning at nine," he said.

DeeDee was indignant when she learned what was developing. "I think I'll go down and talk to the police myself," she exploded. "They ought to know you wouldn't do anything like selling drugs. You don't even drink or smoke."

"Nobody has accused Del and Doug of anything yet," Danny broke in. "Among the authorities, I mean."

"Somebody ought to tell them that those other kids are lying to protect somebody else."

As soon as they finished dinner that evening, DeeDee went over to Nicholsons' to tell Tina what had happened. They prayed together, asking God to intervene in the charge that had been made against Del and Doug. They prayed, too, for the other kids involved, that God would work in their lives and deliver them from the terrible habit that was beginning to enslave them.

"And, dear God," DeeDee prayed, "help them all to confess their sin and put their trust in You to save them."

At the police station, Danny and the boys were

ushered, one at a time, into a private interrogation room, where the same police officer who had taken their story before questioned them again. He asked them separately the same questions. He asked them when and where they met Kurt Nordland and how they came to be invited to the party. They told him about the ski lessons Kurt promised to give them. Then he went to the specific charge that had been made against them. He wanted to know if they had ever used drugs, what they had been doing the three or four nights previous to the party, and how long it had been since they had been to Denver.

They had only been to Denver once, they told him, since moving to Rock Point. At that time they had gone with Danny and Kay to shop for clothes and had been with them all the time.

After a while, he frowned thoughtfully. "That seems to be about all I have to ask you right now. There may be a little more information we'll need later. If there is, I'll get in touch with you."

"Then we're free to go?" Doug asked.

The officer nodded. "Yes, you're free to go." He smiled faintly. "We called you in because of the charge that has been made by two of the kids who were arrested at the party, but your stories check out perfectly. And they check with your reputation back in Fairview. You see, I got in touch with the authorities there after talking with Mr. Orlis on the phone. The county attorney, the sheriff, and the school superintendent all assured me that there has to be some mistake unless you boys have changed radically from what you were when you lived in Minnesota. It all adds up to a clean record."

They thanked him and left.

"Well," Danny said, the relief evident in his own voice, "I guess it wasn't so bad after all."

"No, but I was scared," Del said. "I don't mind telling you that. I thought we were headed for jail for sure."

"Kay and I were concerned too," Danny answered. "In fact, we spent most of the night praying. And you know, God answered our prayers in a wonderful way. It was your own reputations back in Fairview that made them see that you couldn't be involved."

Del and Doug went back to school, missing out on no more than the first period. Chuck Grover and Ernie Stein saw them in the lunchroom that noon.

"Hi." Curiosity gleamed in Chuck's eyes. "I didn't know whether you'd be around here today or not."

"How come?" Doug asked. "Did you think we'd be sick or something?"

"In a way. I looked for you first period, and you weren't here."

"We had a little matter to attend to at the police station," Del replied. He had thought that he would be arrogant and resentful when he talked to Chuck. That was the way he felt the night before. Now, however, he had no feeling of dislike or anger toward the other boy, even though he knew Chuck wanted to get him and Doug in trouble.

"Like what? Finding out that they're onto you for pushing?"

"A couple of the guys told them that we had sold them the drugs they were using at the party, but when the police talked to us, they believed us."

Stein refused to accept that. "You're lying!"

"You'll find out soon enough," Doug said mildly. "They checked with the authorities back in Fairview and decided that we were telling them the truth."

Chuck grabbed Stein angrily by the arm. "Come on! They were born lying."

* * *

Del and Doug went to basketball practice every afternoon. Mr. Nelson divided the squad into teams and had frequent scrimmages, shifting players from one position to the other in an effort to find the right combination. He started Doug at guard, moved him to forward briefly, tried him at center in spite of his lack of height, and put him back at forward again. Some of the guys complained bitterly about not getting to play at the position where they wanted to, but that did not bother Doug.

"I'm not getting uptight about where I go," he said, "as long as the coach doesn't point to the door and tell me to use it."

"But I've always played forward," Doug's companion complained. "I even played forward last year on the reserves. Now he shoves me back to guard, and I never get a chance to shoot."

Doug laughed. "You wouldn't get to shoot if you don't get to play either. Don't forget that."

Doug was well satisfied with the way the basketball season was progressing, but Del had some serious doubts about their ability even to make the squad.

"Neither of us has had a chance to play with the first string yet," he reminded his brother as they walked to the library one chilly, early winter evening.

"That's one way of looking at it. Another way is to look at the two cuts in the squad that we've survived. We've still got a chance to get in there as long as we're suited up. I'm sure not ready to give up on it yet. Not until we have to quit."

The week of the first game, the coach made his selection of the starting five.

"But I want you guys to know – all of you – that this is just for the Friday night game. I may go with the same five all through this game, and I may stay with them the next game, but I'm not making any promises. Nobody's got a position for good. To do that, a guy has to keep on producing."

Del got to play with the reserves Friday night and Doug suited up with the first string. He thought he would be riding the bench for the whole game when the third quarter ended without his getting in at all. Midway in the final period, however, one of the forwards fouled out, and Doug was put in. He was tense and made a few mistakes but managed to hold down his position acceptably.

When the game was over, he took Danny and Kay home so he could use the car to take Tina to the snack shop for a submarine sandwich.

She was excited about the game and the fact that he got to play. "I was so proud of you," she said.

In spite of himself, he beamed. She sounded as though she really meant it. That was enough to make him feel good, whether she was right or not.

"I was clumsy out there for a while," he answered. "To tell you the truth, I was scared Coach Nelson was going to give up on me and jerk me out before I settled down."

"You didn't look clumsy to me."

They continued to discuss the game while they ate. They were just finishing when Doug saw Ernie Stein sitting across from them. The big, raw-boned senior flushed as he saw Doug looking at him and got to his feet hurriedly. He muttered something to his companions and went out.

There was something about Stein's manner that disturbed Doug – something furtive and ominous.

"Are you about finished, Tina?" he asked impulsively.

"I guess so." She noted the odd tone of his voice. "Is there something wrong?"

"I'm not sure."

He picked up the check and paid it at the cash register. The two of them hurried out.

"What is it?" Tina asked.

"I don't know, but I've got a funny feeling about Stein." He spoke guardedly. "Danny's car is out there, and I'm afraid he might try to do something to it to get even with us. He threatened Del and me, you know."

They hurried across the street in the direction of their parked car.

"Look!" Tina cried as they got close enough to see the back of the vehicle. "Somebody's under it!"

"Hey there!" Doug shouted, dashing forward.

Whoever was under the car scrambled from underneath it, leaped to his feet, and sped away. Doug chased him about fifty yards but lost him in the darkness. Panting heavily, he came back to where Tina was standing.

"Do you suppose that was Ernie?"

"I haven't got any way of proving it, but I bet it was. There's only one other guy I know who would do anything to our car, and he wasn't at the Snack Shop tonight."

Tina did not question him regarding the other person. She knew whom he was talking about.

"Are you going to call the police?"

"I'm going to see if anything's been damaged first."

He crawled far enough under the car to inspect the left rear wheel, but there was no sign that there was anything wrong. Actually, Doug did not know what damage anyone could do to a car from the position they found Stein in, short of fastening a bomb there. Even Chuck or Stein would not do anything like that.

Satisfied that everything was all right, he and Tina got into the car and pulled away from the curb.

"I don't know about you, Doug," she said, "but I'm frightened."

"There's nothing to get upset about. They probably are just trying to bug us."

They were almost home when a police car pulled up behind them, his light flashing on top of the car.

"I wonder what that's all about," Doug murmured, pulling over to the curb.

The officer approached him crisply. "Are you Douglas Davis?"

"That's right."

"Step out of the car, please. And you, too, young lady."

They did as they were told, even though Doug protested. "What's this all about?"

"Do you object to our inspecting your car?"

"Of course not. Go right ahead."

The officer stayed with them, while his companion got down on his knees and shined his flashlight under the left rear fender.

"What are you looking for?" Doug asked.

"We'll let you know if we find it."

Satisfied there was nothing at the rear of the car,

the officer continued his examination. He looked under the front of the vehicle, opened the hood, and took out the seat cushions. Two or three cars went by slowly while the search went on. After ten minutes, the police detective joined his companion.

"There's nothing in the car. It's clean," he said. Then he turned to Doug. "A report came in earlier this evening that you had been seen making a pickup, and the stuff was taped under the left fender in the tire well. It's obvious that there's nothing there and hasn't been. We're sorry to have inconvenienced you."

Doug did not think about Ernie Stein or the incident at the car a few minutes before, but Tina said, "That must've been Ernie."

"And you frightened him away, eh?" An accusing tone crept into his voice. "It seems as though our informant was a little off on his timing."

"I had nothing to do with that!" Doug protested, his voice rising. "I don't know what Ernie Stein, or whoever it was, was doing under the car. If he was putting drugs there, he was doing it in an effort to get me into some big trouble."

The officer made a notation in his book.

"I'm going to let you go home for now, but we will be in touch with you later."

Doug Davis cringed. It was not Tina's fault, of course, but she had sure made him look guilty. He could see that now. And all because he hadn't remembered to tell the police about the guy under his car.

He saw it all now. Someone called the cops and told them Doug had made a drug pickup. Then Stein, or someone, was supposed to have planted it on the car. The scheme had not worked, but he was in almost as much trouble as if it had. He felt sick and weak inside.

CHAPTER 9

COMPOUNDED IMPLICATIONS

Doug told Danny and Kay and Del about the police search as soon as he got home. They recognized how serious it could be, but Danny did not think it would cause them any more trouble. The police had seemed so convinced before that neither Del nor Doug had anything to do with selling drugs.

"This isn't the kind of evidence that convicts people of crime," he told the boys. "It's all circumstantial, for one thing. And there is some questionable guessing on the part of the detective. The story he worked out sounds plausible, but a number of other plausible stories could be developed too."

"Yeah," Del said, "like somebody's trying to frame us."

"That's one possibility. And I'm sure that Stein will be asked some pointed questions about that when they talk to him."

"Do you think they will talk to him?" Doug wanted to know.

"If I were an officer, I'm sure I'd want to get the answers to some things that aren't clear in my mind. Of course, there's no real evidence against him either. You saw him look at you funny and go outside. A minute later, you caught somebody under your car. You don't have any proof that it was him."

"I know that, but I've sure got a strong suspicion."

That night, before going to bed, the family grouped around the dining table to pray about the bad situation Doug and Del were in.

In spite of Danny's reassurance, Doug was still apprehensive about being called to the police station for further questioning. After they went to their room, he told Del he would not be surprised if they were even arrested.

"That's a happy thought," his brother retorted. "You sure know how to cheer a guy up, don't you?"

"It doesn't make me any happier than it does you, but I saw the look on that detective's face when Tina told him about the guy we chased away from Danny's car. I thought he was going to take me down to the station and lock me up right then."

The way Del saw it, the police already had the word of the two kids who claimed he and Del sold them the drugs for the party at Kurt's. With this choice bit of evidence, they just might think they had enough to make an arrest and try them. "I wouldn't be at all surprised if they'd come around tomorrow or Monday with a warrant for both of us."

"'What're we going to do about that?" Doug asked.

Del shook his head. It was easy to talk about proving that they were not guilty, but how could they do it? If the police could not find the real pusher with all the help they had, how could he and Doug hope to do anything? And, aside from proving they had not done it – he did not know how *they* could find the guilty guy. All they could do was pray, and there were times when even that did not seem as though it would do any good. Del and Doug did not talk about their fears to Danny and Kay or DeeDee, but that weekend their trouble with the authorities was never far from mind. Every time the phone would ring or a car stopped out front, they were sure it was for them.

The police did not call or come after them, however, and they began to relax a little. As far as they were able to learn, the detective had not called Ernie Stein to the station either, but they could not be sure of that. The police would not advertise the fact that they questioned any particular individual unless they had enough evidence to arrest him.

"Every day that goes by without our hearing from the cops is that much better, I'm thinking," Del observed.

"You've got a point there," Doug replied, "but

we won't be sure we're not suspected until the real pusher is caught or the trials are over."

The next few days, Del and Doug heard nothing at all about the drug case. They saw Chuck Grover in the halls at school or hobbling out to the parking lot on his crutches. For some reason they reached the school about the same time he did every morning.

At first Chuck rode to school with Ernie Stein or one of his friends. Lately, however, he had his own car, and got somebody to drive it for him. Usually it was Ernie Stein or Kurt Nordland. When he saw Doug and Del, he always waved, or, if they were close enough, he stopped to talk to them, in spite of the fact that he had only contempt for them.

"There go our little Jesus boys." Bitterness came out clearly, as though there was a certain stigma attached to the designation.

Del and Doug grinned at him without comment. It took more than a remark like that to disturb them.

"How's the leg today?" Del asked.

"What do you care?" Then, before they could answer, he continued. "Oh, that's right. I forgot. You're the church's little helpers. You make everybody want to be Christians by being so sweet and kind. You even pray for Stein and me, don't you?"

Usually Doug was able to control himself, but this particular morning, Chuck was beginning to get to him. "Yes," he said edgily. "We've been praying for both of you."

"Now don't lose your temper," Chuck warned him. "You're supposed to be an example of kindness and love, or did you forget that?"

"You're right, Chuck. I shouldn't lose my temper. I'm sorry."

"You're forgiven. Now you've got another brownie point. Wasn't that nice of me?"

There was no use in talking to him, they decided. He only wanted to ridicule them.

"We ought to take 'em apart, Chuck," Stein muttered. "We ought to get even with them for what they did to Kurt."

The Davis boys pretended they did not hear what Chuck's companion said, but his harsh voice burned into their ears as they walked away.

"That guy!" Doug exclaimed. "He never lets up, does he?"

"You can say that again." He shifted his books from one arm to the other to open his locker. "He's almost as bad as Chuck about getting on our backs and staying there."

Doug nodded. "We sure made an enemy out of Chuck when we cornered him about giving DeeDee such a bad time up at the dude ranch last summer."

"That doesn't bother me any," Del retorted. "Any guy who'd let a character like that torment his sister doesn't amount to much. Chuck deserved everything we said to him and more."

His brother expelled his breath slowly. "I guess I

didn't say anything to him I wouldn't tell him now if it happened again."

That noon Doug had lunch with Tina Nicholson again. The first time it happened was by accident. This time he planned to sit with her. He had wanted to tell Del about it all morning, but for some reason he could not bring himself to do so. Even now, he had difficulty finding the words to inform Del that he would not be sitting with him at lunch and why.

He held back until Tina came into the lunchroom. Then he left his brother abruptly. "I'll be seeing you, Del."

"Hey, where're you going?"

But Doug was already halfway across the floor.

"Hi, Tina." He knew Del was watching him and would probably give him a bad time when they got home that night, but he did not care. Let Del talk about it if he got any fun out of that. It did not bother him any.

"Hello. Where have you been keeping yourself?" Her voice made music out of the words.

"Around."

They entered the line together.

"Did the police call you again?" she asked fearfully.

He shook his head. "We haven't heard anything from them yet."

"I was so sorry about–about what happened the other night. I felt sort of guilty for telling the detective about the guy doing something to your car."

"You did the right thing. I'm the one who should have told him. I didn't mean to keep it from him, but I didn't think about it at the time."

They got their food and found a table. Tina was about to choose one closer to the line of traffic, but Doug led her off to one corner. He was not going to have his brother come by with a pocketful of wise cracks if he could help it.

Del looked over at him and smirked, but that was all. He made no move to come over and let loose with that corny act of his. Doug was glad about that.

"I was so worried about you Friday night that I wasn't able to sleep," she told him. "I must have prayed for you most of the night."

For some reason, that made him feel good, beyond the fact that he appreciated her prayer. Doug had never supposed Tina would really be concerned about him. She must like him a little bit or it would not have made much difference to her one way or the other.

* * *

At the next basketball game, Mr. Nelson had Doug suit up with the reserves. He was not too surprised at that. He had been so upset the last week or so that he had not been able to play as well as he usually did. In spite of the fact that he could understand why it had been done, however, he was still disturbed by it.

"I thought I'd get to suit up with the first team

again," he complained to Del. "I know I've been off a little this week, but I don't think I've been that far off."

"I thought you'd be with the first string again too," Del said, "but I didn't figure I'd do any better. I'll tell you one thing, it's rough to make the first string in any sport when you go to a school as big as this one."

Doug straightened thoughtfully. "I'm still going to make the first string. I don't care what anybody says."

Del laughed good-naturedly. "I thought you didn't care what team you got to play with or what position the coach decided to use you in, as long as you got to play."

"That's right." Doug spoke defensively. He did not like the gleam in his brother's eyes.

"What happened? Did Tina tell you how much she *adores* first string basketball players?"

"Very funny."

"I can see her now. She gets that sweet, winsome look on her face, and those blue eyes get as big as coffee cups, and she says, 'Oh, Douglas, I do hope you can get to play on the first string. I'll be so proud of you!'"

Doug's face flushed. "Can it, wise guy! Nobody's laughing."

"'You will make the starting lineup for little old me, won't you, Douglas?'"

"I'm warning you, Del!"

But he did not stop. "I know how it is, Doug. I understand," he said in mock seriousness.

"Just you wait!"

He laughed again. There was nothing he enjoyed more than razzing his brother, especially about something that got to him the way kidding him about Tina did.

* * *

The following week, Danny and Kay were invited to a wedding in Fairview, Minnesota. DeeDee decided she would go along to see some of her old friends who still lived there. Del and Doug could have gone too, but they were having a difficult time hanging onto their places on the basketball squad as it was. If they went to Fairview and missed a few days' practice, they would be finished for sure.

"Besides, most of our friends are gone," Doug said. "It wouldn't be much fun for us to go back there."

It was only a coincidence, the boys knew, an ugly combination of circumstances nobody was responsible for, but the morning after Danny and Kay and DeeDee left for Fairview, Del and Doug were called to the police station. A plainclothes officer appeared at the principal's office, told him what he wanted, and had the two Davis boys sent down from their English literature class.

The instant the teacher dismissed them, they glanced uneasily at each other and got to their feet.

"What do you suppose this is all about?" Doug said softly when they were out in the hall.

Del shrugged. He did not know for sure, but he had a good idea. There could only be one explanation.

When they reached the office and saw the detective, their hearts beat fiercely, and their mouths were dry and coppery. They said hello to the officer, but he did not return the greeting.

"I think it's time we have a serious talk at the station," he said.

"But we've already told you everything we know," Doug protested.

"I prefer to discuss the matter at the station," the detective continued.

"But Danny isn't here now to be with us."

"I'm well aware of that. We contacted him by phone this morning. We have his permission to talk to you."

This time the atmosphere at the police station was different than before. The officers were courteous enough to Del and Doug, but their hostility showed through. It was apparent that they believed the Davis boys had lied to them.

The detective had a recorder in the interrogation room. After advising them of their rights and asking permission to record their answers, he flicked on the machine and began.

Many of the questions were the same as those they had answered before, only this time the police pressed for more and more details. He reminded them repeatedly that they would have to tell the truth or things would go much harder for them.

"You might as well know that we have quite a good case against you already, and we are continuing our investigation. Things will be better for all of us if you will tell us the truth now."

"But we *are* telling you the truth," Doug protested.

That seemed to make the officer angry, and he separated them for the balance of the questioning. Sweat gleamed around Doug's hairline as the officer continued the questioning in a sharp, accusatory voice. He cracked all of his knuckles and fumbled with one corner of his shirt collar.

But, for all his nervousness, his story did not change. The detective shot the same questions at him time after time, rephrased and in a different context, but the answers were always the same.

After an hour or more, the police interrogator gave up. "Perhaps your brother will be a little more cooperative," he said.

Doug did not reply, but he was not concerned that Del would say anything different than what he had said before. They were both telling the truth; so there was no reason for changing their story. He waited in the station for them to finish with Del.

The detective followed Del to the door.

"I'm not going to make a formal arrest now," he said, "because our investigation isn't complete. But I have already informed Mr. Orlis that you are strongly suspected. If the rest of our investigation substantiates what we've already learned, we will have no choice but to turn the evidence over to the county attorney. When we do that, he will file charges."

A junior officer drove the Davis boys back to the school and let them out. He tried talking with them a couple of times, but when they failed to answer his questions, he too fell silent.

Once they were alone, Del faced his brother. "This is rough," he exclaimed.

"I kept telling that detective the truth," Doug said, "but he wouldn't believe me."

"So did I."

They went into the school to class, but they might just as well have stayed home. They did not hear anything that was said, and they both flunked a history quiz miserably.

CHAPTER 10

FOILED AGAIN

When they went back home that evening, after the poorest showing they had made in basketball practice since they went out for it, Tina's dad came out to talk to them.

"I'm glad you boys are home," he said. "The police were just here."

They stared at him. "T-they were?"

"I would have called you at school, but I didn't think there was any need of getting you all upset. Betty saw the thieves trying to open the back door with some keys they had. She called the police, but the thieves got away."

"Did they get in the house?" Del demanded. "Were they able to steal anything?"

He shook his head. "No, she happened to come home at the right time. I suppose they figured we would take them for repairmen Danny and Kay had given the keys to so they could go into the house and fix the washer or dryer or maybe the TV.

But she talked with Kay just before she and Danny left, and she mentioned being concerned about burglary. Kay asked Betty to keep an eye on the place. When the guys ran away, she knew they must have been trying to break in."

The boys thanked him and went into the house.

"That's strange, isn't it?" Doug mused.

"You mean somebody trying to break in at this particular time?"

"I suppose it could be a coincidence, but it sure seems funny."

They went into the family room.

"Let's take a look at the whole thing," Doug began, sprawling in an easy chair. "We're accused of pushing drugs by two of the kids who were caught at Kurt's party. We're asked to go down to the police station for questioning, but they believe us because of our reputations. Right?"

"Right." Del laid down on the floor on his stomach.

"Then Tina and I see Ernie Stein – or someone – lying under the back of Danny's car when we come out of the snack shop, but we chase him away before he gets a chance to do anything. Before we get home, the police stop us and search the car. And where's the first place they look? Under the left rear fender. They had an anonymous phone call that I had picked up some drugs and that's where I hid it on the car.

Then we're called in and questioned closely. When the police can't get us to change our stories, they say they are still looking for evidence to link us with the drug pushing. Now someone tries to break into the house when there's nobody at home. What does all of that say to you?"

"I've been doing a lot of thinking about it myself," Del said, "but the police wouldn't come here without a search warrant and when nobody's home to look for evidence."

"I know that. But did it ever occur to you that the same guy or guys who tried to frame me by putting the drugs on the car would be trying to do the same thing here at home?"

Del got to his feet, still tugging at the lobe of his ear. He had not thought of that before, but now that Doug mentioned it, it did make sense.

"They may have gotten some evidence we don't know about into the hands of the police," Doug continued. "That could be the cause of that interrogation we had yesterday. And when that wasn't enough, they tried to break into the house in an effort to plant some more evidence here."

"You just could be right." The more Del considered it, the surer he was that Doug did have the affair figured out. It was the only explanation that brought the whole picture into sharp focus. It was the sort of deal that guys like Chuck Grover and Kurt Nordland

and Ernie Stein might cook up. "But what are we going to do about it?"

"It won't do any good for us to go to the cops now," Doug said. "They would think we concocted the whole scheme to get ourselves off the hook. They'd never believe us."

"The way I see it, we're going to have all we can do to keep from getting in deeper than we are already. The cops are convinced now that we're guilty. If they'd find some drugs in the house or in our lockers at school, they'd throw the book at us, and there wouldn't be anything we could do about it."

The more they considered the matter, the more determined they were to keep a close watch until Danny and Kay got back and they could find out what else they could do to clear themselves.

"Why don't we go visit our youth pastor tomorrow?" Doug suggested.

"Before or after they find the drugs planted somewhere?" Del retorted. "We have to do something *tonight.*"

They talked it over at length and decided they would have to keep watch both at home and at school. Drugs planted in their lockers would be equally as serious as finding it in their room at home.

It was decided that Doug would remain at home and watch for intruders while Del would go down to Northwest. He parked on a side street a couple of blocks from the school and made his way to the end of the building where their lockers were located. He sought a place in the thickest shadows and sat down to wait, pulling his knees up under his chin.

He was not at all sure one guy would be able to watch a whole building the size of Northwest High. It was a huge, sprawling structure with two floors and lots of glass. Anyone with a flashlight in an outside corridor would risk being seen. If he stayed in the inner halls, the chances were better that he would be able to avoid detection.

At home Doug turned on the lights the way he normally would if he suspected nothing. He went through the motions of studying in his room and went to the kitchen for something to eat. The thing he really dreaded the most was turning out all the lights and going to bed. He would be sleeping in the very room anyone attempting to plant drugs on him and Del would be sure to seek out. He felt uneasy being alone in the huge house.

Del has it even worse, Doug reasoned. *He has to stay out in the cold, watching for someone who might never come.*

At the school, watching the windows by the lockers, Del shivered and pulled his coat's hood up over his head. Standing guard had sounded sensible when he and Doug talked about it earlier in the evening. Now, however, as the chill night wrapped its arms about him and the wind knifed through his coat, he wished he were home in bed. Of course, Del figured, this was better than spending the night alone in that spooky house.

He had been there for at least two hours but had seen nothing. To be sure, he could watch only one door, but he tried to tell himself that he should be able to see the flashlight a person in the vast building would have to have to find his way to their lockers. The corridors all had long glass panes in the doors and windows on all the outside walls. He should be able to see anyone who approached their lockers with a light.

Another hour passed, and the cold seeped up into his feet from the snow and crept into his legs and knees. He stood up and began to walk back and forth as quietly as possible to increase his circulation. And then he saw a faint pinpoint of light in a second floor window.

He stiffened, staring and holding his breath.

The light had only been visible for a second. Now that it was gone, doubt gripped him. It could have been his imagination, prodded by the cold and his anxiety to be done with the whole business.

Then he saw the light again, moving slowly along the hall near their lockers.

Someone *was* inside! Now all he had to do was call the police and their worries would be over! But what if they did not believe him? What if they were too slow getting there? What if the police cars scared the guy away? Now that the character was inside, it would only take him a few minutes to open their lockers and do what he'd come to do! If that happened, Del knew that he and Doug would be in deep trouble.

He had to go in there and stop him alone – if he could! With an unuttered prayer in his heart, Del dashed to the back door, tried it, and found it open. As stealthily and as hurriedly as possible, he sneaked up the back stairs and turned to the outside corridor. Whoever was there still worked at one of the lockers so intently he heard nothing.

Del crept forward. He was a dozen steps away when the prowler heard him. He stopped working on the lock and spun around, swinging his flashlight high, probing the darkness. He found Del with it an instant before the Davis boy tackled him, sending a crutch clattering across the tiled floor. Del and Chuck went down together.

"You!" Del cried, getting to his feet and grasping Chuck by the arm.

"I can explain," Chuck whimpered. "You hurt my leg again! And this time you hurt it bad!" He rubbed the spot where he had broken it before.

Del wrenched the flashlight from his hand and got his crutch.

"Just what were you doing at my locker?" he demanded.

"I wasn't in your locker."

"Maybe not, but you were sure *trying* to get into it."

"I came back to get some books to study for a

quiz tomorrow," Chuck murmured desperately. "I must have gotten to the wrong locker. I didn't mean anything by it."

Del was scarcely listening. He swept the wall with the flashlight.

"What're you looking for?" Chuck asked.

"For *this!*" The beam revealed the fire alarm handle.

"Don't, Del! Please! I'm on probation this year! Don't turn me in!"

Before he finished pleading, Del had broken the glass with the crutch and sounded the alarm. Three or four minutes later, the fire department and the police were there.

"I can explain," Chuck said over and over. "If you'll just give me a chance, I can explain everything."

"You'll have your chance," the officer said, helping Chuck to his feet. In searching him, he came across two folders of white powder and a box of forty capsules. "Unless I'm badly mistaken, these are heroin."

"He planted them on me!" An accusing finger pointed at Del. "It's all his fault."

The officer acted as though he had not even heard him.

* * *

Del and Doug were asked to go down to headquarters to tell the police everything that happened. When they got there, however, the officer in charge told them he did not need them.

"Grover made a complete confession," he said, "of everything. If you've got a minute, I think you're entitled to know what was going on. Chuck had urged Kurt Nordland to plan the party and to get you two there on the pretext of teaching you to ski. What Kurt didn't know was that Chuck also made an anonymous call to our vice squad tipping us off to the party. That's how they came to raid it that particular night."

"You mean *he* got the party going and then called you so it would be raided?" Doug asked in amazement.

"That's right. He really must've had it in for you two. He said he thought Kurt's dad had so much pull with the department as mayor that he'd be able to get him off. You two are the ones he was after."

When that had not worked, Chuck got a couple of the guys who were at the party to say they bought their drugs from Del and Doug. "When that did not work, he started trying to get evidence planted on you to make us believe you were pushers. He had Ernie Stein try to plant it on the car and later at the house. When Ernie couldn't get the job done, he decided to go to the school himself and do it. He had stolen a key to the back door as well as a master key to the lockers in this corridor. He thought he had everything worked out, but I guess he didn't count on you figuring out what was going on and waiting for him.

Del and Doug only shook their heads sadly.

The officer seemed surprised that the boys took no delight in the trouble Chuck was in. "After all," he said, "Grover tried his best to frame you. And he almost got away with it."

"But he didn't. That's all that really counts."

"Besides," Doug said, "we've just found out what it's like to be in trouble with the law. We feel sorry for anyone who has to go through it, even if he deserves it."

At school the next day, talk of Kurt Nordland's drug party burst out again in spite of the fact that it had all but vanished from conversation around the halls in the long weeks since the arrests were made. The story of Chuck Grover's involvement raced through the student body.

When the trial was held, everyone was found guilty as charged, and Kurt and Chuck and Ernie were tried and found guilty of the most serious charge and would undoubtedly receive the stiffest sentences. The news came first as Del and Doug were leaving school following basketball practice. Hank Warren wheeled over to the curb and rolled down his window.

His voice was taut with excitement. "Guess what! The judge found them all guilty!"

Del and Doug leaned over by the car. "Are you sure?"

"I just heard it. I didn't think they'd ever nail Chuck!"

"Neither did he."

The other boy reached over and opened the door. "Hop in. I'll give you a lift where you're going."

"Thanks."

They crawled in beside him. He still could talk of little else as they drove home through the growing gloom of the evening.

At the dinner table that night, the entire family was excited about the trial.

"You took a crazy chance, Del, doing what you did," Danny reminded him.

"I had to. If I hadn't gone in there, Chuck would've gotten away with it!"

"What do you suppose the judge will do to Chuck?" DeeDee asked.

Danny was not sure. "The news reporter said that he was going to postpone sentencing for a month to allow time for the probation officer's investigation, but I have a feeling that the three ringleaders are going to have to serve some time in the detention center or maybe wait until they're eighteen and go to prison. The charges are too serious to give them more probation."

"I wish there was some other way of punishing them," Doug said.

"So do I." For a time Del was silent. "But, you know, the one I really feel the sorriest for is Ernie Stein. I'm afraid Chuck and Kurt talked him into helping."

"Of course, that's no excuse," Danny reminded

them. "When we break the law, we have to be punished by the law."

"I'd like to go over and talk to him just the same."

"So would I," Doug added.

Ernie was home alone when they knocked on the door. He had been sitting in the living room with the lights off. Even the TV was dark and silent.

"What do you guys want?" he demanded sullenly.

"We'd like to talk to you."

"I don't feel like arguing with you about what we – about what I tried to do to you. I've about had it for today."

"We didn't come to talk to you about that," Doug said. "One time when you were with Chuck, we told you that we have been praying for you. We came over to tell you that we still are."

He stared at them. "After what I did? Are you some kind of nuts?" It did not make sense to him.

"Tonight we came over to tell you that we love you and Jesus Christ loves you."

Ernie stepped aside wordlessly to allow them to come in.

Sitting on the couch, one on each side of him, they went through the "Four Spiritual Laws" booklet with him. They were praying with him as he confessed his sin and gave his heart to Jesus Christ when his parents came in. When Doug and Del got their coats to leave, Mr. Stein and Ernie followed them to the door.

"Do you suppose you could have somebody come and talk to the wife and me?" Mr. Stein asked.

"We'll have Danny call our pastor as soon as we get home."

"You do that. I never used to think there was anything to this Jesus business. But if He can make guys like you come here to try and help Ernie after what he tried to do to you, there's got to be something to it!"

There was a spring to the boys' step as they went out to the car. "If only Chuck Grover would trust Christ now, everything would be wonderful."

"We'll keep praying for him," Del answered. "He'll accept Christ. It may not be for a while, but we're praying for him and so are his uncle and Scot and who knows how many other people. God will answer those prayers. We can count on it."

"Maybe this is what it will take to reach him." For the first time, Doug began to feel good about what happened. Not that he was glad Chuck would be sentenced to the detention center, but that God could work even through circumstances like that to bring about His will.

When they reached the house, Kay was on the phone. "Oh, here they are now." She handed the phone to Del. "It's Mr. Knight."

"Hello?" Del said.

"Just read about the flying tackle you made in the dark one night."

Del laughed. "Well, my brother and I have played

football for three years; I *should* be able to knock down a guy on crutches!"

"Why don't you two make a special effort to come back out for the team next fall?"

"Thank you, Mr. Knight!"

"I'm not making any promises; I just wanted you to know I'd be proud to have boys like you on my team."

THE DANNY ORLIS SERIES

The Danny Orlis series, by Bernard Palmer, delivers a blend of adventure, mystery, and suspense through various settings—from the Canadian wilderness to Guatemalan jungles. Danny Orlis, an adept outdoorsman, skilled athlete, and committed Christian, employs his quick thinking, calm bravery, and biblical solutions to confront everyday problems and hair-raising dangers. Early stories focus on Danny navigating school life, sports, and outdoor challenges, while in later books, Danny and his wife Kay provide wisdom and guidance to youngsters facing lifelike situations and challenges. Having sold over two million copies, this series has made Palmer a renowned author in Christian youth literature. Palmer is also the author of the Felicia Cartright series and various other series for Christian youth.

AVAILABLE FROM WWW.ANEKOPRESS.COM